J
and o

Fifteen heartwarm
published in Th

CW00421788

Just the ticket

"Are you all right there, love? Is there anything I can help you find?"

Claire was crouched low on the floor of the charity shop, browsing the books on the bottom shelf. She steadied herself against the bookshelf as she stood, one of her knees giving an embarrassing crack.

"I'm just looking for something good to read on my holiday next week," she smiled at the shop assistant. "I've picked three novels, so I think that'll be enough to keep me busy for a while."

"Are you going anywhere nice?" the assistant asked, as she rang the books through the till.

"No," Claire sighed. "I'm not going away, but at least it's a week off work. I'm just planning a few quiet days at home."

The problem was there were too many quiet days at home. In fact, the past few months since Claire and Paul had split up, life had been just a little bit too quiet.

"Well, I hope you have a really nice break," said the assistant. "And enjoy your books!"

Claire lifted the three novels from the shop counter and dropped them into the flowered canvas bag slung over her shoulder.

Back at home in her flat, Claire sat with her feet up on the sofa and her favourite mug, filled with tea. She took the three books from her bag and turned each one over in her hand.

One was a cosy crime story, the second was a whodunit and the third was a romance. She read the blurb on the back of each book, each one followed by quotes from newspapers and famous authors. "Sensational!" one of the quotes read at the back of the cosy crime. She picked up the romance novel. "Unputdownable!" it screamed. Was that even a real word, Claire wondered. She flicked open the pages of the whodunit and as she did so, a small piece of flimsy, salmon coloured paper floated down to the floor. She reached down to retrieve it. It was roughly the shape and size of a five-pound note. But it wasn't until Claire picked it up and held it in her hand that she realised what it was. It was a ticket, a football ticket, for a game that had been played over 20 years ago. And it hadn't been used, the tear-off portion at one end was still attached, the perforations intact. Whoever had owned the book before her must have been using the ticket as a bookmark. Claire rang the charity shop and asked if they kept details of where their donated books came from. But her desire to return the football ticket to its owner came to nothing when the voice at the other end of the shop said that they didn't keep details like that. Claire looked at the ticket.

Aston Town vs Shelford AFC
Regional Cup Final
Saturday 7 May, 1994

It seemed a shame to throw it away, especially when it hadn't even been used. Claire wondered if a collector might want it, and within minutes she had started up her laptop to browse the internet.

With every search that she did for that particular football match, pictures of the Aston Town goalkeeper Jimmy Montez kept appearing. She remembered Jimmy Montez from all those years ago, he was on TV a lot back then, and in the newspapers too. With his good looks, masses of long dark curly hair and winning smile, he always seemed to be photographed with a leggy blonde at his side. She could faintly remember reading that Jimmy Montez married one of those blondes, many years ago. Intrigued to know more, Claire clicked on a headline: *Jimmy Montez wins the cup for Town!* Aston Town had won the cup final against Shelford AFC back in 1994. The score was one-nil, with the winning goal scored by Jimmy Montez. He was feted as the local hero, and took pride of place on the team's open-air bus when it toured Aston Town to celebrate the win. Claire didn't know much about football, she didn't watch it on TV and had never been to a game, so the ticket she'd just found meant nothing to her. But she knew that for such an important game there might be someone out there who would welcome the addition to their collection.

She opened up an internet auction site and listed the ticket for 99p, just enough to cover the cost of a stamp and envelope to post it to whoever bought it. Claire decided that whatever money she raised from the sale of the ticket, however small, she'd pop into the box at the charity shop.

As the week went by, Claire checked daily on the progress of the ticket auction. There had been no interest, not one single bid.

Then just when the auction was closing, in its final seconds, a bid of 99p appeared. She'd sold it! Someone actually wanted the ticket! It was an auction bidder called Meg56 who had bought it. Payment for the ticket appeared immediately into Claire's account, along with the name and address of a woman who had bought it. It was a local address, one she could reach easily with just a short bus ride from her flat. Claire emailed back, suggesting that she would be happy to hand deliver the ticket rather than send it through the post. Within seconds she received a reply:

Thankyou. That would be lovely. I've bought the ticket as a surprise for my son. He'll be over the moon when he sees it.

Claire emailed back:

I'm free to bring the ticket to you any time next week

Well, what else was she going to do with her week off work? And again, immediately, a reply was received.

Monday morning? 10am?

Claire replied:

Great, I'll see you then!

After a quiet weekend with just her parents for company at Sunday lunch, Claire found herself looking forward to venturing out on Monday at the start of her week's holiday.

On the bus journey to the address she'd been sent from the auction site, Claire wondered who the little boy was who would be receiving a new addition to his football ticket collection. She found the address quickly and walked up the avenue admiring the three-storey houses, set well back from the road behind their long gardens. She stopped outside No. 15 and pushed open the wrought-iron gate, closing it behind her. The garden path was bordered on both sides with masses of flowers and shrubs, and a well-tended lawn stood to one side. There was a large bay-window next to the front door. Claire knocked, and waited.

The door was opened and a woman who Claire placed at around the same age as her mum welcomed her inside. Claire guessed that the lady might be the boy's grandmother. "Hello, you must be Claire," the lady said with a welcoming smile. "Come in, please." Claire stood in the entry hall, taking an envelope from her canvas bag.

"Have you time for a cuppa?" asked the woman.

"Oh, I won't stop," Claire said. "I've got the ticket here…"

"Ah, now there's a shame. The kettle has just boiled and I've baked some ginger cake, it's still warm from the oven."

"Well, only if you're sure?" Claire said.

"I'm sure," she replied. "I'm Margaret, by the way. Or Meg56 as you know me by on the auction site."

"Oh, *you're* Meg56?" Claire tried to keep the surprise from her voice, but realised she might have failed.

"I am indeed," Margaret smiled. "I keep up to date with all the internet things, you know. Not just the auction sites. I enjoy looking at maps from all over the world and I talk to my sister in Australia on the webcam. I love it."

"I was just…" Claire started to say. "I thought you said it was your little boy you'd bought the football ticket for?"

"My son, yes. He'll be ever so happy when he finds out what I bought for him online."

Claire handed over the ticket in the envelope to Margaret as she followed her through to the kitchen. The smell of warm ginger cake wafted towards them both down the hallway.

In the kitchen, Margaret busied herself with the kettle, cups and plates for the cake. "Have a seat, dear," she said, and Claire took her place at one of the chairs around the oak dining table. Margaret placed the tea pot and three mugs on a tray on the table. Then she brought three plates to the table, each with a generous slice of soft, caramel coloured cake. She caught Claire's puzzled glance.

"Oh, sorry dear. That third plate's for my son. He should be here any minute." Margaret picked up the envelope from the table and peered at the ticket inside. "He is going to be so pleased, I just know it. I can't wait to see the look on his face."

Just then there was a sound at the front door. "Here he is now," Margaret said, her face beaming. Claire watched as the athletic build of a man strolled into the kitchen. A pair of muscled, tanned arms in a blue t-shirt wrapped themselves around Margaret in a bear hug. "You all right, mum?" her son asked, giving Margaret a peck on the cheek.

"James, this is Claire, the woman from the internet I was telling you about," Margaret said. James reached his hand towards Claire, and she received the firmest of hand shakes. Glancing up, she took in the features of Margaret's son. There was something familiar about him, but she couldn't say what it was. His tanned bald head emphasised his deep blue eyes and he smelled nice too, something citrus and fresh. It was his smile that was familiar, now where had she seen it before?

"Sit down, son, have some cake and some tea," Margaret said. James sat next to Claire.
"What is it you wanted to show me, mum?" he asked. Margaret slid the envelope across the table to James and when he opened it, she couldn't have been more pleased with his reaction when he saw what was inside.
"Oh mum! The match ticket!" He reached out and covered his mum's hand with his own. "And where did you say you got it from?"
"From Claire, here," Margaret nodded.
"I found it in a book," Claire explained. "From a charity shop. But I figured there might be a collector who would want it, as it was from such a special game."
"This means the world to me," James said to Claire. She noticed there were tears in his eyes. He gripped his mum's hand tight. "Thanks mum," he said. "I didn't think I'd see any stuff from that match again. But here it is, here in my hand, finally, a memento of my moment of glory."
Claire's mind whirled. It couldn't be…?

"He lost everything from his footballing days," Margaret explained. "When his wife took off with the gym instructor, she threw out all of his footballing memorabilia, didn't she, James, love?"

James nodded and looked at Claire, a little embarrassed. "Yeah, but mum, we don't have to go into all that again now, do we?"

Margaret nodded. "You're right, son. We don't. That was a long time ago. I'm just happy to have been able to get back a little piece of your past for you."

"And so am I, mum," James said. He turned to Claire. "And I can't thank you enough either. He took a drink from his mug of tea. "Would you let me treat you to lunch out today, Claire, by way of thanks?"

Before Claire could answer, James turned to his mum. "And you mum, the three of us, my treat."

"That'd be lovely, thankyou, James," Claire said.

James gave Claire a disarming smile.

"Please, call me Jimmy," he said.

Last orders, please!

"If the next man who walks through that door isn't tall, dark and handsome, then I'm going for my lunch break," Diane said firmly to her boss.

"That's fine by me," Sandra laughed. "We're not that busy anyway, so you can take your break now if you'd like?"

Diane stood her ground. "No, I'm going to wait and see who the next customer is that walks into the bar. You just never know…"

"Oh, I think we do," said Sandra, glancing over to the door as it swung open and a black collie dog trotted inside.

"It's Patch!" Diane said. "Well, it's a he - and he's dark, I'll give him that but I'm not sure if he's tall and handsome. I might pop out for a breath of fresh air now then, Sandra, if you're sure you can manage on your own for an hour?"

"You go and have your lunch break," Sandra told her barmaid. "I think I'll be able to cope with the mid-day rush."

Diane looked around the pub. It was empty except for the two of them behind the bar and a black collie dog. "If a coach load of American tourists pull up outside and they all come rushing in, and you need me back before half-past, send me a text and I'll come straight back," Diane smiled.

A few seconds after the dog had entered the pub, it lay down beside its favourite seat and curled up to go to sleep. The dog's owner followed into the pub and before he reached the bar, Sandra had already started pulling his favourite pint.

"Pint of the usual, Stan?" she asked.

He nodded in reply.

"June not with you today?" Sandra enquired. It was odd for Stan to come into the pub on his own. He and June had been among Sandra's most regular customers for years. She struggled to remember the last time she had seen either of them without the other.

Stan's face clouded over.

"I've come in here for a bit of peace and quiet," he said, sharply. "And I'd be obliged if you didn't mention that flamin' woman's name!"

Sandra handed Stan his favourite pint of stout, money was exchanged and after she gave him his change, he went to sit beside Patch.

Sandra pulled up a stool behind the bar to sit on, opened her puzzle book, took a pen and started concentrating on a tricky crossword she'd been trying to crack all day. Inside the pub, the only noises were those from Patch as he sniffed by the fire. And then there was the tiniest scraping when every few seconds, Stan lifted his pint, took a sip and replaced it to the table. It had been a very slow day inside Sandra's pub, she knew she didn't even need her barmaid Diane in to help her, but she kept her on during the weekdays, just in case. Sandra liked the pub when it was quiet, but she'd only had Diane to talk to all morning and felt in need of more conversation. She glanced over at Stan who had a face like thunder. But in all her years running her own pub, when had that ever stopped her from chatting to her customers?

"Cold outside today, is it?" she asked in her best friendly voice.

"Aye," Stan nodded.

Sandra tried again.

"The weather man on the telly this morning said we might get a bit of rain this afternoon."

"Is that right, now?" Stan replied, but his tone suggested he really didn't care whether a heat wave or a snow storm might have been on its way.

Sandra went through her mental checklist of neutral questions she'd normally use to quiz her customers. After questions about the weather, the topics could range from programmes she'd seen on last night's television through to the headlines in the local paper. Well, as long as the headlines weren't about politics or the local council, as those subjects could always be relied upon to raise voices and tempers. She decided to ask Stan if he'd like to try the new local beer that the brewery were asking her to promote in the pub. But just as she was about to try, yet again, to engage Stan in some form of conversation, the pub door swung open again.

"Afternoon, Mick," she said as she greeted her customer with a smile. "Pint of the usual, is it?"

Mick put his hand into his jacket pocket and Sandra could hear the jingle of loose change. She saw him glance down at the coins in his hand.

"Just a half, please, Sandra," he said. "I'm having to tighten my belt, money-wise, at the moment."

"Still no luck with your job hunting, then?" Sandra asked. She pulled the pump handle slowly down and beer filled up the glass.

Mick shook his head.

"I'm going to take my drink and go through some more job sites on my phone for an hour or so. See if I can find anyone that's got some work for an unemployed gardener."

"I hope you find something soon, Mick," Sandra told him.

Mick handed over the exact amount of money, all in coins, for his small glass of beer. He headed to the other end of the pub, away from where Stan and Patch were sitting in companionable silence.

Sandra went back to her crossword and just when she thought she had cracked one of the clues, the pub door swung open again. She looked up from her puzzle to see Stan's wife June standing at the bar, bristling.

"If you happen to see my husband in here today," June announced to Sandra, loud enough for Stan to hear her. "Can you tell him from me that there will be no dinner on the table tonight until I've had an apology from him."

Sandra glanced from June to Stan and back again. She noticed that Stan looked unmoved by the arrival of his wife, his gaze not shifting from the patch of wall he was staring at.

"Are you having a drink, June, while you're here?" Sandra asked her.

"I might as well, it'll help me keep an eye on Stan over there."

"Your usual orange and lemonade?" Sandra asked.

"Might as well put a splash of gin in too," June sighed.

After Sandra had served her, June took her drink and sat at the other side of the bar from where Stan was seated. Sandra felt like a referee, squarely placed in the centre between the warring couple.

In all her years of knowing them both, she'd never seen them like this before. She glanced at her watch and wondered where Diane had gone on her lunch break. Then she decided to tackle her crossword again and after a few minutes she started filling in some of the blank squares in the grid that had foxed her so far. When the pub door swung open again, it was a man whom Sandra had never seen before.

"Hello there, what can I get you?" she asked.
"Is that the local beer, that one there?" the man asked, pointing to one of the beer clips on the bar.
"The brewery's been promoting this one a lot," Sandra said. "It's quite nice, seems to be going down well, very popular with the locals."
"I'll have a pint, thanks," he replied. "And I don't suppose you know the quickest way to get to the post office from here? I'm new here, my wife and I have just moved onto the new estate down the hill. I'm still trying to find my way around."
"There's a post office on the main road," Sandra said. "It's only a short walk from here."
"Thank you," he replied. "I'll have to pop up there this afternoon, there's so much to sort out when you move house, isn't there? Forms for all sorts of things have to be sent off. And I was hoping it might be the sort of post office where I could put a card in the window. We desperately need someone to come and help us sort the garden out. It's great having a new house on a new estate, but underneath the top soil the garden's full of builder's rubble. It's like prospecting for gold looking for decent soil there."

Sandra handed over the pint to the newcomer.
"How much do I owe you?" he asked.

Sandra shook her head, and pulled a second pint too. "These are on the house," she said and she pushed his pint towards him across the bar. "This one's for you as it's your first visit to what I hope will be your local pub… and do you see that man sitting over there, the one using his phone?" Sandra nodded towards Mick. "Well, this pint's for him. Why don't you take these drinks and go and have a chat. I think he might be just the person you need to help you find your garden gold."

After an introductory handshake, the man and Mick were soon deep in conversation. Sandra briefly toyed with returning to her crossword but felt there was something more pressing she needed to do.
She went back to the bar and pulled another full pint of Stan's favourite stout. Then she mixed up an orange and lemonade in one of her fanciest glasses with another splash of June's favourite gin. She added a cherry on a cocktail stick and a paper umbrella to the drink. She took the pint of stout and laid it on the table in front of Stan.

"That's from June. She doesn't want a fuss, but she says she's sorry and it'll never happen again."
"Aye," Stan nodded. "Least said, soonest mended."
Then Sandra went back to the bar, and took the fruit cocktail to June.
"That's from Stan. He's asked me to send it over to you."
June sniffed when she saw the drink in front of her.
"He says he's sorry," Sandra continued. "And he's sent this by way of an apology."
"Well, it's a start, I suppose," June sighed.

"Oh, and he says that he doesn't want the matter mentioned ever again," Sandra added as she walked back to the bar. When she reached her stool and took up her puzzle book again, she saw from the corner of her eye the slightest movement from Stan. He raised his glass to June, and although she didn't change seats to move closer to her husband, Sandra was happy to see June raise her glass in return. It was the sight of Patch who brought June from her seat to sit at Stan's table. And it wasn't too long afterwards that June and Stan ended up sitting side by side. When they rose to leave the pub, Stan brought their empty glasses back to the bar.

"Cheerio," he grumbled to Sandra as he and June left the pub hand in hand, with Patch by their side. Mick also left the bar with a smile on his face, and the address of his next gardening job in his pocket. And finally the newcomer left the pub too, determined to find the post office and get to know his new village.

"Ooh, it's getting chilly out there," Diane said as she returned to the pub. "Looks like the weather man on the telly this morning was right after all. We might get that rain this afternoon."
"Have a nice lunch break?" Sandra asked.
"Just had a quick walk to the shops and back," Diane replied. "Did I miss much in here while I was gone?"
Sandra smiled and turned back to her crossword. "It's been quiet," she said. "Nice and peaceful. And that's just the way I like it."

Mixed Signals

"It says here you should meet him somewhere public," Julie said, reading down the web page. "It should be somewhere that you can leave easily if you need to."

"And you should leave details with a friend," Wendy chipped in.

"And never go home with someone you've just met," Julie added.

Sue rolled her eyes. "I'm not intending to go home with anyone. I'm only meeting him for a pizza."

"We're just looking out for you, Sue," Wendy said as an idea struck her. She shot Julie a look. "Actually, why don't me and Julie go with you?"

"It's a blind date, not a girls' night out," Sue laughed. "And it's not even that blind a date, really, I've been emailing Paul for weeks. And it's a reputable dating website we met on. I'm sure I'll be fine."

Julie shook her head. "Wendy's right. You need us there, just in case Mr. Online turns out to be Mr. Off His Rocker. You can never be too careful, Sue. Someone who can be bright and witty and seem perfectly normal online, may prove to be very far from that in real life. We'll sit quietly at a table where we can keep our eye on him for you. We're coming with you whether you want us or not."

After some planning, Sue finally decided that she wouldn't be able to convince her friends otherwise. Since her painful divorce, Wendy and Julie had been there to help her get through it, they'd helped her every step of the way.

She knew they were being protective because they didn't want to see her hurt, but coming along on a date with her, well, the logistics were going to take some working out.

"Right, so this is what we'll do," Sue told her friends. "You two can sit at a table that's not within ear-shot of me and my date. But it'll have to be a table where you can see me clearly. Then, we'll work out a code where I can communicate to you how the date's going, without having to speak or use my phone."
"What, like waving the napkin if you want us to leave?" asked Julie.
"I was thinking of something more subtle," Sue replied. "If the date's going okay, I'll give you the thumbs up sign."
"Thumbs up means ok," Wendy typed into her phone.
"And if I'm unsure and I want you to stick around a bit longer, I'll rub my nose up and down, like I'm scratching it, right?"
"Nose rub means hang about," Wendy typed.
"What if you need our intervention, immediately?" Julie asked.
"I'll play with my right ear," Sue said. "And that's your cue to ring my phone, which I'll have on the table with me, just in case. When the phone rings, I'll answer it and pretend I'm listening to an emergency call from home and then I'll tell Paul I have to leave right away."
"Right ear, emergency," Wendy typed.
"And if it's going really well and you want us to leave?" Julie asked.
"I'll rub my left ear."

"Left ear, leave," Wendy typed. "I've got them all in my phone, Sue. Thumbs up means all is OK. A nose rub means you're unsure. Rubbing your right ear means you need help and rubbing your left ear means you want us to leave. I think we're all set. So, which pizza place are we going to tonight?"

"It's the one in the high street. I'll go in first, find Paul and get seated and then once you see where we're sitting, you two come in and sit at a table close by. But not *too* close, right?"

Wendy and Julie nodded.

"I don't want to feel as if you're eavesdropping on my date. I know you're worried about me and you want to look after me and I love you both dearly for that. But I need a bit of privacy, got it?"

"Got it," Julie and Wendy chimed.

That evening, when Sue entered the restaurant, she scanned the tables looking for a man who fit the description Paul had given her online. She'd seen his pictures on the dating website, but she knew how misleading those pictures could be. The first profile picture she'd ever used had been taken when her hair was much longer and lighter than it currently was. She was much slimmer then too. Once she'd got to know Paul after their weeks of emails and texts, she'd sent him a current photo. And Paul had responded to her email with a smile and an extra kiss at the end, so he must have liked what he saw.

The pizza restaurant wasn't too busy and it was easy to spot a table where one man sitting alone. He had his back to her and she walked over to him, noticing his mass of dark, curly hair.

Sue walked slowly, nervously, her heart thumping in her chest. When she reached the table she looked down at the man who was staring intently at the menu. She gave a little cough.

"Are you Paul, by any chance?"

He smiled up at her. It was a lovely smile, Sue thought. First impressions were good, he looked normal, and kind and quite friendly too.

"Sue? It's lovely to meet you," he said, extending his hand. "I've been looking forward to this."

He stood and pulled out a chair for Sue. She settled herself into the seat, taking off her coat and positioning her phone on the table by her side. She looked again at Paul, taking in his features as fully as she could.

"I have to admit I'm a little nervous," he said, running his fingers through his thick, dark hair. "I've never been on an internet date before."

"Me neither," Sue said. "But I've eaten here before, with my friends, and the pizzas are amazing."

As Sue and Paul studied the menus and made small talk about the weather and the traffic routes they'd taken. Sue spotted Wendy and Julie walking in. She kept a discreet watch on them both as they positioned themselves at a table not too far away. They were in full view and she smiled when she caught Julie's eye. Happy that her friends were in and could be called on if needed, Sue turned her full attention to Paul.

Across the restaurant, Wendy and Julie were watching carefully.

"I don't believe it! Julie! I don't believe it!" Wendy whispered across the table.

"What?"

"I've lost my phone. It's not here. I had it this afternoon when I was at my mum's… oh Julie. I've left my phone at mum's. And it's got Sue's secret code signals in it."

"Don't worry," Julie said. "I'm sure we'll remember them. Thumbs up was okay, wasn't it? What were the others? Nose rubbing meant something, didn't it? And one ear was the emergency ear and the other ear was the one that means she wants us to leave. Oh crikey, we'll never remember which is which now."

"We'll just have to do our best," Wendy said. "Watch her face. Is she still smiling?"

As carefully as she could, Julie turned her gaze towards Sue and Paul's table.

"Yes, she looks happy enough, she's chatting away to him."

"He looks nice, doesn't he?" Wendy said and Julie nodded in agreement.

"Seems a bit nervous though, don't you think? He keeps running his fingers through his hair."

"Nice hair, though," Wendy said. "We'll have to keep our eye on her now. If she stops smiling or she looks distressed, we'll swoop over to their table…"

"Swoop? We're not exactly Cagney and Lacey, said Julie.

"Well, I'll swoop and you can walk behind me. And then we'll give Mr Online a right ear bashing, leave him to pay the bill, rescue Sue and take her home."

"Oh no… talking about ear bashing, she's doing it, look!" whispered Julie. "Sue's rubbing her left ear. Is that the emergency ear?"

"I can't remember, Julie, but we can't take any chances!" replied Wendy. "Ring her, Julie, ring her!"

Sue's phone buzzed into life on the table. Before she picked it up she glanced over at Wendy and Julie's table where she could see her two friends in a state of panic.

"I really should have turned the flaming thing off," Sue laughed. "Sorry about this Paul. I'll quickly take this call if you don't mind, it might be important. It's from a friend, you see, who… er… she's been ill."

"Sue?" Julie breathed down the phone. "You ok, hun?"

"Fine thankyou. Wrong ear," Sue replied quickly and hung up.

"Does she need me to swoop?" Wendy asked Julie when she told her what Sue had said, but Julie just shook her head.

Wendy and Julie looked over at Sue, who was deep in conversation with Paul. Every now and then their conversation would break into laughter.

"Whatever it is Sue's just told him must be really funny because he's crying with laughter," Julie said.

"How do you know?" asked Wendy.

"He keeps dabbing at one eye with the napkin," Julie said.

"She seems okay. I think we should let them get on with their date," Wendy said. "We'll check on her in a few minutes, all right?"

Julie agreed, and they started to study the menu, ready to order their meals. The next time they glanced over at Sue and Paul, Sue gave her friends the thumbs up sign and a very broad smile.

"Ah, the universal language of the thumb," Wendy said to Julie. "That one's easy to understand."

And as they watched Sue sitting at the table giving her friends the sign that all was going well, they noticed Paul was doing the same thing too. Wendy looked in the direction of Paul's gaze and sure enough, across the room, at a table not too far away from Sue and Paul's were two men eating pizza.

"No!" whispered Wendy to Julie. "I don't believe it! Look over there!"

The two women stared at the men across the restaurant. In return, the men stared back at Wendy and Julie.

"Paul's been doing the same thing as Sue," breathed Julie. "He brought his mates too. That's what all that running his fingers through his hair and dabbing at his eyes was all about. He's been signaling too!"

"I'm going over there to have a word with the pair of them," Wendy said. And before Julie could stop her, Wendy was striding across to their table. Julie had no choice but to follow her, just in case things got out of hand.

Sue watched, gobsmacked, as Wendy and Julie slid into the seats around the table to sit with the two men. She saw the four of them shake hands as introductions were made and then they started laughing and chatting. And the next thing Sue knew, she saw them call the cocktail waitress over.

"Those people over there, at that table…" Sue said, wondering how much she should tell Paul about bringing Wendy and Julie with her on their date.

"I'm sorry about bringing them," Paul said.

"Who?" Sue asked in surprise.

"My mates, Dan and Mick. I was so nervous about meeting you, so we devised a code where I would let them know if I needed their help. If you and I weren't getting along, I would scratch my nose and they'd come and rescue me. If I ran my fingers through my hair it meant all was okay."

"You see those two women that they're with? They're my friends," Sue admitted. "They insisted on coming, said I needed looking after."

Sue and Paul turned and looked across the restaurant to where their friends were raising a toast with their cocktails. Wendy, Julie, Dan and Mick turned to meet their friends' gaze. Each of them held a cocktail in one hand, and with the other hand they gave the universal language of a thumbs-up sign.

The Dating App

"Could I get you a drink, madam?"

Susan smiled at the barman and gently shook her head.

"No, it's all right, thank you. I'm just waiting for someone."

The barman gave a discrete nod and walked away to serve another customer as Susan checked her watch, again. Phil said he'd be here at eight and it was twenty past now. Maybe he was having trouble parking, Sue thought. Or maybe he'd decided not to bring his car after all and had travelled into town on a bus that was running late. Another five minutes went by, then ten. Susan checked her phone but it was all quiet on the Phil front with no messages or texts from the man she was due to meet; the man she'd been looking forward to meeting for weeks.

"Are you sure I can't get you anything while you wait?" the barman asked again. Susan watched as he straightened bottles of spirits on a glass shelf and then he turned back towards her.

"I could rustle up one of my special cocktails for you, if you'd like?"

Susan shook her head.

"No, thank you," she said, checking her watch yet again. But when she saw it was quarter to nine, her shoulders dropped and she let out a long sigh.

"Oh, go on then," she said. "I might as well. I'll give him the time it takes me to drink one of your cocktails and then I'm giving up and going home."

"Your boyfriend is it?" the barman asked and then quickly he shook his head, looking flustered.

"Sorry... that was nosy of me, forgive me. What I meant to say was…"

"Well, it was a bit nosy, but no, he's not my boyfriend," she laughed. "Although I was kind of hoping he might be. I met him online, you see, and tonight was going to be our first proper meeting." Susan checked her phone again but there was still nothing. Well, she wasn't going to message him if he couldn't be bothered to even let her know why he was running late. She'd been certain he'd turn up, ever since they'd agreed to meet in real life after finding each other on a dating app. She'd been using the app for months but Phil was the first man she'd met who had ticked all her boxes, in every way.

The app pronounced them a perfect match. According to the app, theirs was a match made, well, if not in heaven, then certainly online. She liked the way he looked in his profile picture, his strong handsome face and his muscled shoulders. And he said he liked the way she looked too, although to be fair, it was an old picture that showed her in her favourite dress and in a flattering light. After the mutual attraction came the online questionnaire they'd both had to fill in. And Phil's questionnaire was an exact match for her own. He liked all the things she did, all of them, even the walks in the country, the horse riding and visiting art exhibitions. And she liked all the things he did too, every single one. He even had a dog, a big shaggy dog called Freddy and Susan loved dogs, the shaggier the better. He couldn't have been more perfect. But where on earth was he now? Why hadn't he turned up for their date?

They'd been chatting about their date, messaging and texting for weeks now, planning exactly the kind of date that Phil said was his favourite – and one that Susan agreed she loved too. They'd planned to meet in the new wine bar in town, have a drink and a chat and then move on to the Italian place for a bit of romance over two plates of risotto, their favourite food. Susan had even bought a new dress in the exact shade of blue that she and Phil both agreed was their favourite. She checked her phone again, it was almost nine o'clock but there was still no message from Phil who was now officially an hour late.

"Madam?"
The barman offered Susan a hardbacked booklet with the pages inside covering all kinds of wonderful cocktails. Some of them she recognised the names of, but many of them were new to her. She laid the menu down on the bar and fully settled into her seat for the first time that night before removing her coat. She laid it on the bar stool next to her, just in case Phil turned up very late.
"There's so many to choose from I don't quite know where to start," she smiled. "Surprise me!"
"Perhaps you'd allow me to create a new cocktail especially for you," he said. "It's a passion of mine. I love creating new cocktails and naming them too."
"That sounds wonderful," she replied. "Just one thing… none of that liquorice liqueur please, I'm not keen on that."
"Oh, that's one of my favourites," he said. "But, as you wish, I'll leave the liquorice well alone."

The barman set to work, pulling a large flat glass from the shelf and then he stood back from the bottles of spirits and liqueurs, stroking his chin, wondering which ones to use.

"Let me know what you think…" the barman said at last when he slid the glass along the bar towards Susan.

"Sorry," Susan said. "I was miles away there, wondering where my date was."

"Has he stood you up?" the barman asked.

Susan nodded. "It appears so," she replied. "And we seemed to have everything in common, too. Do you know how rare that is, these days?"

She lifted the frosted glass to her lips and took a sip from the cocktail within. The barman watched and waited for Susan's response. But she couldn't speak, not at first, as the sweet fizzy liquid played on her tongue and dazzled her taste buds.

"It's beautiful," Susan said at last. "It's absolutely gorgeous. What did you say this one's called?"

"I didn't…" the barman replied. "I haven't named it yet. It's a new one I've created. I've been playing around with different flavours for a week now and it's taken me a while to get it right."

"Well this is stunning," Susan said, taking another sip. "I know nothing about cocktails, so this is all new to me but it really is fantastic."

"Perhaps you'd like some nibbles to go with it?" the barman suggested, and he brought another small menu towards Susan. She glanced at it quickly, trying to work out what was what but it was difficult as it was written in Spanish and she didn't understand a word.

"I'm terrible with menus," Susan said. "My trouble is, I'm not a great cook and I've got no sense of what food goes with what wine. I can't even cook very well and rely on ready meals at home…"

"Then let me help," the barman smiled. "This one will complement the cocktail better than say, this one," he suggested, pointing at the second and third items on the list.

"Then I'll be guided by you," Susan smiled. "Thank you…?"

"Tom," he replied.

Susan sighed again.

"I can't believe Phil hasn't turned up. You think you know someone, eh?"

"Ah, but how well can you know them when you've never met them?" Tom said sagely.

Susan shrugged.

"I've missed an episode of EastEnders to come here tonight. Mind you, so has Phil, or at least he would've missed it if he'd turned up. That was one of the things we liked about each other, one of our matches was that we liked the same soap on TV."

"I'm more of a Coronation Street fan myself," Tom replied. "Always have been."

Susan took a sip from her drink.

"I was going to take him horse riding at the weekend, if he'd turned up, of course."

Tom shook his head.

"Horses? I'm terrified of them. And don't even get me started on cows!"

Susan laughed.

"What about something smaller then, like a cat or a dog?"

Tom's hand flew to the back of his neck.

"I'm allergic," he said, shaking his head. "Just the thought of being in the same room as a dog brings me out in a rash. Mind you, I like sea birds. Beautiful things they are, flying out over the ocean. I spend most of my spare time at the beach, with a pair of binoculars in my hand, twitching."

"Sorry?"

"Twitching," he repeated. "Bird watching. When I'm not working, that is. Mind you, I love my work here. I help the chef create the bar menu and keep it fresh. I've got a knack for knowing which food goes well with the drinks."

"Well, you'll get no complaints from me on that score," Susan said, taking another sip of her drink. Then she helped herself to one of the large, stuffed olives that Tom had placed in a bowl in front of her.

"They're Spanish olives," he explained. "I love Spain, the food… the people…"

"Never been," Susan said. "I prefer Italy."

"So, what do you like doing when you're not horse riding or waiting in bars for unreliable men?" Tom smiled.

"Oh... I like art," Susan said eagerly. "I love visiting exhibitions, seeing new paintings, discovering new artists."

"Nah, that's not my cup of tea," he replied. "I don't know anything about art."

"Neither do I," Susan laughed. "I just like what I see… I don't think you need to understand what you're seeing in an art gallery, not really. You just have to like it, appreciate it. And if you don't like it, you move on until you see something you do."

"I don't think art galleries are my type of place, somehow. Bit too posh for my liking," Tom said.

"The one in town isn't posh," Susan smiled. "You should go sometime… I'll go with you if you like. Sorry, I wasn't being pushy. I mean, just if you want to."

Tom was about to reply when Susan's phone buzzed into life on the bar top. She saw Phil's name on the screen and swiped the message open that he'd left. He hadn't even bothered to call her, he'd just sent a text, a very brief one at that.

"Everything all right?" Tom asked. Susan held out her phone so that Tom could see the message from Phil.

"See that? It says he's not coming. He doesn't give a reason, he doesn't even give an excuse. Just says he'll catch me online soon. Well, he's got another thing coming."

Susan pressed and held Phil's message and then swiped it into the trash can on her phone. "There, that's it. He's gone. I've deleted his number from my phone so I'm not tempted to ring him back."

"Maybe I could make you another drink?" Tom offered.

"Just one then," Susan replied. "And then I'll get a cab home. What a waste of a night it's been."

"Not entirely," Tom smiled. "We've got a visit to an art gallery to look forward to together. That is, if you meant what you said, about taking me there to show me some art?"

"Suppose we could…" Susan replied. "If you're free one afternoon?"

"Here, let me offer you another cocktail," Tom said.
"On the house this time as you've been kind enough
to try my new cocktail tonight. It hasn't even gone on
the bar menu yet, but if you think it's good
enough…"

"Oh, it's good enough," Susan said, draining her
glass.

"… then I'll put it on the specials board tomorrow
night and see how it goes."

"You'll need a name for it, won't you?" Susan asked.

Tom thought for a moment.

"Do you know," he said, smiling at Susan. "I think
I'll call it *Opposites Attract*."

Whatever the Weather

"And now, with today's weather for the region, it's over to our weather presenter Diane."

Bob the newsreader kept his smile on his face for the camera before it panned across the studio to Diane, waiting by her weather board. Diane had been delivering the weather news on her local television station for the last 12 years. And in all those years, she'd predicted many long hazy summer days and plenty of rain showers. She'd even forecast her share of snow storms and blizzards and once, a hurricane too. Diane had stood in the same studio, in front of the same weather board, for all of those 12 years. A true professional, there had been days when she had struggled into work to deliver the meteorological news when she'd been feeling under the weather herself. But today was the first time she'd had to deliver the forecast with a broken heart.

"It's very overcast and cloudy out there today," Diane smiled into the camera, hoping that her voice wouldn't crack with the wave of emotion she felt instead. "We're seeing a cold front arriving from the west, bringing in a wet and windy depression. So do take care out there, as the heavy rain warning is in place for the rest of today."

The camera panned back to Bob behind his news desk.

"Thank you, Diane, for the weather. And we'll be back with you this evening with a round-up of your local news."

The cameraman raised his right arm in the air.

"And… we're done!" he yelled.

Bob removed his microphone and stood up from behind the news desk. He glanced over at Diane. "Are you all right, Di?" he asked her, concerned. "You seemed a little shaken, there, doing the weather today."

"I'm ok," she lied, and before Bob could pry any further, she left the studio quickly. She decided to head to the canteen to have a coffee before she returned to her desk. When she saw her friend and colleague Kate sitting by the window in the café, she headed to sit beside her with her hot drink.

"Hey!" Kate said, looking up from her phone when she spotted Diane. "Have you heard from Ian yet?"

Diane shook her head. "I think we're finished, Kate," she said.

"You're giving up too easily," Kate said. "He's a smashing bloke, Di. You know we all think the world of him."

Diane stirred her coffee, swirling the frothy milk around the cup with her spoon.

"I know… everyone tells me we're such a good match."

"Then what on earth do you keep pushing him away for?" Kate laughed. "If we can all see how happy he makes you, what's stopping you from letting him into your life?"

Diane sighed. She'd been over and over this for days in her head and still couldn't make sense of it.

"He wants us to move in together, Kate," she said. "And I'm just not ready for it, not yet."

Kate raised an eyebrow. "And you've told him all of this, have you?"

Diane nodded. "Ian thinks I'm against the idea because I don't love him, not because I'm…"

"…scared?" Kate suggested.

"You know me too well," Diane smiled.

"Can I give you some advice?" Kate said, and without waiting for an answer, she pointed to the large television screen on one of the canteen walls. If I were you I'd plaster that smile on a bit more brightly next time you go on air to give the weather forecast."

"Did it come across on screen how awful I'm feeling inside?" Diane said.

"Afraid so, kid," said Kate. "There'll be emails from the viewers complaining, if you're not careful. You know how much they like you. You've been the cheerful weather presenter at the station since before some of our viewers were born."

"Thanks Kate," said Diane. She drained the rest of her coffee and headed slowly back to her office. She wasn't due back on air for a couple of hours and Diane knew that she had to clear her head and concentrate on her work. When she entered the open-plan office she shared with the rest of the news team, Jake the sports presenter caught her eye as she walked past his desk.

"You've had a delivery," he said. "It's over there, on your desk. Came in while you were on air."

Diane glanced over to the corner of the room where her desk was tucked in by the window. And as she walked towards her desk, she saw a hand-tied bouquet of white tea-roses mixed in with purple freesias, her two favourite flowers in all of the world. There was only one person who knew her favourite flowers, and sure enough the note confirmed that Ian had sent them. The note attached simply read: *I love you.*

Diane logged on to her computer to catch up with work emails. Then she checked the latest meteorological reports in order to prepare her next weather slot she would give later that afternoon. She tried to lose herself in her work but her thoughts kept returning to Ian and their argument the night before. He wanted them both to live together, for Diane to move into his flat, but she knew she wasn't ready. She had been hurt in relationships before and wanted to tread slowly this time.

"You can't keep shutting me out because of your past," Ian had told her, begging her to reconsider. "And I could be your future, if only you'd let me… if only you'd trust me." They'd talked over this all night, going round in circles and finally Ian had stormed out, leaving Diane in tears. She'd barely slept and now her mind was still whirling with thoughts of Ian, as she sat at her desk and prepared her next forecast. Diane decided to put the flowers into water. She headed towards the kitchen where she found an old vase to keep them in until she could take them home at the end of her shift. When she was back at her desk, the perfume from the roses and freesias lifted her heart with every breath that she took. Soon, it was time for the local news and weather to go out live once again. Diane and Bob headed to the studio and Diane took her place in front of the weather board, as she always did.

"The rain looks set to move away to the east with the depression starting to lift," she said, pointing with her left hand to the weather board. "And we might just see a break in the clouds with a slight improvement in the temperature by the end of the day."

When Diane returned home that evening she found a large, light blue envelope lying on her door mat. The envelope had no stamp and only her first name had been written on the front, Clearly someone had pushed it through the letter box while she'd been at work. Without even taking off her coat, Diane sunk down onto her sofa, slit the envelope open and pulled out a sheet of traditional, cream, heavy writing paper. It was a letter, from Ian, and not just any letter but an old-fashioned love letter. He didn't say much, but what he did say struck Diane to the core and made tears spring to her eyes. He wouldn't push her, she read. He would wait for her, wait for her as long as it took because he loved her and wanted nothing more… nothing more in the world than to be with her.

That night, Diane slept better and arrived at work the next day in a much more positive frame of mind. "Across the middle of the region we'll start to see some hazy sunshine this week," she smiled at the camera, "…and we might just be able to put those umbrellas away for a little while too. The temperature should be a couple of degrees warmer than we've seen lately and the weather looks set fair to be a lot more calm than of late. And now it's back to Bob on the news desk."

Bob smiled to the camera, said his goodbyes and he and Diane waited for the cameraman to give them his usual signal to tell them they'd gone off-air. Diane headed straight back to her office as she was due in a team meeting before her next forecast later that day.

And as she approached her desk, she saw another small bouquet, this time it was a single red rose nestled inside a small bunch of white freesias. She lifted it toward her and breathed in the heady scent. Taped to the brown paper and string wrapping of the bouquet was a tiny white envelope which Diane ripped open. Inside, in Ian's handwriting were just two words in a question - *Saturday lunch?* After her team meeting, Diane sent a text message to Ian to accept the lunch date and Ian suggested they meet in her favourite Italian restaurant in town. Then she decided to put all thoughts of Ian to one side, as best as she could, and concentrate on her work and the weather. Diane knew that once she got home that evening she would have plenty of time to think about what to say to Ian and what to wear for their date. She knew she didn't want to lose him, they made each other happy and she felt settled with him in a way she'd never felt before. But she also knew that she had to make him accept she wasn't ready to move in with him, not yet. Once she had prepared her afternoon forecast, Diane walked down to the studio and on her way there, she caught up with newsreader Bob in the corridor.

"You're looking a bit brighter," Bob told her.

"I'm feeling a bit sunnier, that's true," she replied.

After Bob finished reading the news, it was time for Diane to read the weather forecast for the coming weekend.

"It looks like we've got a few days of some lovely weather coming up, folks," Diane said to the camera on her next weather slot.

"And if you're out and about this weekend, there could be some spells of calm and very pleasant weather with some bright rays of sunshine too. But if we do get any rain this weekend, especially on Saturday when the sun will beak through, keep a look-out for rainbows. They always appear when you least expect them."

Saturday's lunch date came and went and Diane was happy with the way things had gone. She'd been firm with Ian and although she had told him she loved him, she'd made it very clear she wasn't ready to move on to the next step, not just yet. In return, Ian didn't try to make her change her mind, this time. He said over again that he'd wait for her, and promised that he'd wait for as long as it took.

"And in the meantime, let's relax and enjoy our relationship," said Diane, raising her glass of red wine.

Ian raised his glass too. "I'll drink to that," he smiled. "So the short-term forecast is… sunny and warm, you might say?"

Diane laughed. "I'd agree with that," she said and then raised her glass again. "And the long-term forecast looks very promising too."

The Orange Blossom Holiday Tour

Nicolas, the coach driver, sees the group coming before I do.

"Here they are," he tells me when he spies them in his rear-view mirror. I leap down from the coach, straighten my navy blue skirt and adjust the orange bow tie that I'm obliged to wear for work. Flaming orange! It's the one colour that I know doesn't suit me and does me no favours at all. As soon as I see my colleague Helen heading my way with the party of tourists behind her, I switch on my meet and greet smile.

"Dazzle 'em with your dentures, Sue!" Helen whispers in my ear as she passes me her clipboard. She always tries to make me laugh when we do these handovers but I'm too professional to give in to the giggles when I'm working.

"Hello everyone," I greet the throng of holidaymakers. "My name's Sue and our driver is Nicolas. Once Nicolas has taken your suitcases from you and stowed them safely in the coach we'll be on our way to the hotel."

It's a well-worn drill on the airport pick-ups. I do it every week in my job as a holiday rep for the Orange Blossom Tour company. We're in southern Spain, where the orange trees grow and where, this time of year, the air is sweet with pungent white blossom. It's a scent I adore and one I never want to get used to. The orange trees grow in the streets and in the parks here, and breathing in the scent from the small white flowers is a joy. I take the orange blossom tourists to visit churches and castles and give them a real flavour of Spain.

"Could I sit behind the driver, dear? I get travel sick if I don't sit behind the driver," a woman's voice tells me when I'm checking off names as the passengers board the coach. I turn to see a short, older lady fanning her face with her hands to try to ward off the intense Spanish heat.

Most of the holidaymakers look tired, their faces as crumpled as their clothes after hours inside the airplane. The flight here from England is only three hours but I know that their day would have started far earlier than that with taxis to the airport, queuing at check-in and then waiting, some of them nervously, in the departures lounge. I know and understand how tired and disorientated most of them will be so I don't bombard them with too much information when we meet for the first time. I smile and nod and say 'hello' and 'how are you?' and 'welcome aboard'. I am as helpful, polite, and professional as I can possibly be with an orange nylon bow tie tickling my neck.

A woman, about my age, is next to board the coach. She's another one who looks tired but there's something else about her I pick up, she looks sad too, miserable in fact. My heart goes out to her. "Amanda Wilson," she tells me quietly and I check off her name on the clipboard. "And my husband's Paul. Paul Wilson. He's just putting the case in the coach with your driver."

She turns and points to a man who is trying to help Nicolas put their suitcase in the coach.

But Nicolas is determined to do it himself. Not only is against company policy to let the holidaymakers lift their own suitcases and bags into the coach, Nicolas has too much macho pride to allow another man to help with his work.

The man that I now know as Paul Wilson is being terribly British, insisting that he help with the suitcase. In return, Nicolas is being typically Spanish and shoos Paul away after heaving the bulky suitcase into the coach. Paul is the last person to board and I've got a tick against every name on my list. Nicolas locks up the baggage hold and takes his seat behind the wheel as I radio in to the Orange Blossom Tour HQ to let them know we're ready to leave. And with that, I jump on board too, make my welcome announcement to the passengers and Nicolas pulls the coach out of the car park.

The journey to the hotel on the fast road, the Autovia, takes one hour. On board the coach the passengers are quiet at first, taking in the sights as the coach thunders along at 120 kilometres an hour. But it doesn't take long for the chatter to begin, the tiredness giving way to the excitement of being on holiday.

I walk up through the coach to ensure everyone is all right, and I hand out maps of the small town in which the hotel is based. Most people welcome the information and greet me with a smile although one or two are asleep.

When I come to the seats where Amanda and Paul Wilson are seated, I see Amanda nervously playing with her wedding ring while Paul remains aloof, looking out of the window as if his life depended on it. As Amanda takes the map from me, we lock eyes for a moment and she attempts a smile.

I give her the denture dazzle, as Helen would call it. "Everything all right?" I ask breezily, ever the professional. Amanda nods in reply but I note that Paul's gaze doesn't move from the window.

The first day of the holiday is a day with no tours, giving the holidaymakers a chance to acclimatize themselves to the hotel and the town. It's a beautiful place, one of the old white towns, one of my favourites in Spain. I used to come here on holiday myself before I fell in love with the place and moved out here for good. The hotel is superb, set high on a cliff top overlooking the sea. It was originally built as a paper mill and was left empty for years after the mill closed down. But now it's owned by the Orange Blossom Tour company who renovated it beautifully. All of the hotel bedrooms have views from their balconies of the blue ocean beyond.

There is not much for me to do on the first day apart from turn up at my allocated time at the hotel, wait in the reception area and see if anyone needs any assistance. I pass the time by chatting to the hotel staff, they all know me now, after all these years. As I chat with Alvaro, the head receptionist in the hotel, one of the holidaymakers walks towards me. It's the older lady from the coach yesterday, the one who insisted on sitting behind Nicolas.

"Is there a chemist nearby, dear?" she asks me. "I've got an awful gyppy tum."

I walk with her to the hotel entrance and point out the direction to the nearest *farmacia* which is just one street away. The rest of the day remains quiet and it is not until the next day that I meet my holidaymakers again.

The first tour of the week is to a nearby village where the castle and church are impressive and of historic worth. The group who board the coach today are far removed from the tired, grumpy, crumpled group who rolled off the airplane just two days before. They're dressed in bright clothes, some wearing hats and sunglasses, with brightly coloured bags slung over their shoulders and their phones are out, ready to take photos. They're all smiling and happy, well, almost all. Amanda Wilson still looks tired, her eyes red as if she's been crying, but it's not my place to comment or ask. I have to remain professional, but still, I can't help but wonder. Paul Wilson is as silent as ever and doesn't even return my good morning greetings as he boards the coach after his wife.

Nicolas sets the coach in motion once everyone is aboard and we soon arrive at the outskirts of the village where we park the coach. Everyone is free to visit the village and the sights on their own, take lunch where they'd like. I ask them to meet back at the coach at the allocated time. Many of them head straight for the castle, some for the cathedral while others make a bee-line for the tapas bar opposite the coach. Amanda and Paul Wilson are last to leave the coach and seem in no hurry to go anywhere.

"Do you need any help?" I ask Amanda as she stands beside Paul by the coach. "Suggestions of places to see, perhaps?"

She looks up at me shyly. "Actually, you could help, yes. Can you recommend anywhere we could go for a coffee? Just somewhere quiet to can sit and talk, without too many tourists?"

I knew the perfect place and shared its location with Amanda.

"When you reach the square, turn left and look for a green wooden door. On the door there will be sign that reads *Mariana.* Push open the door and go in. Tell them Sue from the orange blossom tour sent you." Then I had a second thought. "No… tell them Sue and Nicolas sent you. They'll treat you like an old friend, I promise."

"Thank you," said Amanda and she ran to catch up with Paul who was already striding away.

I knew from many years' experience that Mariana's coffee and home-made cakes could cheer up anyone, well, almost anyone. It would only be the stoniest soul that wouldn't be softened having entered through that green wooden door. It looked nothing from the outside, just a battered door set in an old stone wall. But once inside, there was a tiled courtyard with a fountain bubbling gently in which tiny, colourful birds bathed.

Pots of cool, white geraniums were placed around the courtyard and deep pink bougainvillea tumbled down a wall. In the centre of the courtyard was an orange tree, heavy with sweet-smelling blossom.

There were tables and chairs in the courtyard and the café was ready and waiting. I truly hoped that Mariana's café would work some of its magic on Amanda and Paul, as it had once worked its magic on me.

Finally the time came for the group to assemble at the coach before our return to the hotel. Everyone was on board except two people – Amanda and Paul Wilson. I shot Nicolas a worried look but he shook his head and smiled. "They'll be okay," he said. Sure enough, I caught sight of them walking along the cobbled street towards the coach. My heart lifted when I noticed that they were holding hands.

"Thank you," Paul said to me when they reached the coach.

"Did you enjoy Mariana's?" I asked.

"We did," Amanda said. Paul boarded the coach but Amanda hung back and took me to one side.

"I can't thank you enough," she said. "We came on this holiday because we... well, we've been going through a difficult patch. We thought that coming on a coach tour holiday with lots of other people would be the best thing to do, that it would jolly us along and force us to join in with things. But being on our own today, at Mariana's, away from everyone else, it was just what we needed. We opened up to each other more today than we have done in months. So, thank you, Sue, we really appreciate it."

I put my hand on Amanda's arm and helped her onto the coach.

With everyone seated on the coach, Nicolas strapped his seatbelt around him and readied the coach to leave. Along the cobbled street at the café, Mariana watered white geraniums in pots and put out crumbs for the birds by the fountain. The café was where I had first met Nicolas many years ago, when he was helping his sister Mariana serve coffee and cake to tourists, of which I was one. I had no idea back then that Mariana's café would become the venue for our wedding, where our guests dance and sang under the orange tree festooned with lights. Nicolas and I also have the orange blossom at Mariana's café to thank for playing another vital role in our lives. It was where we decided on the name of our coach holiday tour company.

As Nicolas swung the coach out into the main square, I allowed myself a little smile and adjusted the orange bow tie around my neck, once again.

Tiptoe Through the Tulips

I don't know much about flowers and plants, but I'm surrounded by people who do. Gardening is not only my husband's job, it's his passion too – and it's one my mother shares. However, somehow the gardening green-fingers have passed me by but I get to enjoy the fruits – and veg - of their labours.

When I was growing up, we always had a flower-filled back garden when we were kids. Whatever the time of year, there was always colour and shape to the garden and I remember mum giving talks to local women's groups, sharing gardening advice. When we'd go shopping she would buy packets of seeds and string bags of bulbs mixed in with the weekly supermarket shop.

Having a beautiful garden was something I took for granted. It was something that was always there, something mum looked after. It seemed too much like hard work to me then, and to be honest, still does. When I first met Bob and told mum he ran a plant nursery, she was over the moon. She thought they'd have a lot to talk about, common ground if you like. However, she was wrong.

Bob was an only child, and his parents had long since passed away when I met him. He's a bit of an introvert, if truth be told, and has always got on better with plants than people. I fancied him like mad when we first met at college, although it took me ages to get to know him properly.

He was always so very reserved, as if he had a barrier around him, and he let people get to know him slowly and carefully. I persevered - and I still love him to bits, but there are times when I wish he'd stop retreating into his shell. Because if there's one thing I've never understood it's that he and my mum have never really got along. I mean, they're polite to each other, they're even nice sometimes. But it seems, at times, like a forced friendship. Bob only ever sees mum if I'm there to act as a go-between.

Mum's long resigned herself to thinking of Bob as part of my life, but not part of hers. "As long as he makes you happy, that's all I care about," she says. And he does make me happy, he does. I just wish he'd be more like himself when he's with her, instead of clamming up. When he's in the same room as mum, he's like one of those plants he likes, the ones that close up their leaves on an evening when the sun's gone in.

"How do you fancy a trip to Holland?" Bob asked me when he came in from work one day. "I've been given some tickets from a supplier, it's a freebie. Airfare, hotel, guided tour of the tulip fields and a trip to a flower festival all thrown in for free. What do you say?"
"I say thankyou very much, lovely husband," and I kissed him on the cheek. "When do we go?"
"Next weekend," he said. "I might ask Stuart at work if he wants to come with us."

"Stuart?" I asked, shocked. "But he's only started working with you in the last week and he's not even a gardener, is he? I thought he was just at the nursery helping out on work experience from the local college?"

"But they've given me three tickets," Bob said. "It'd be a shame not to use them all."

"I know someone passionate about gardening who'd give their right arm to come with us," I said.

Bob didn't even need to ask who I had in mind. He just raised his eyebrows and sighed.

And that's how the three of us ended up sitting together on a plane headed to Amsterdam. Well, when I say 'together' … me and mum were sitting next to each other while Bob managed to get an aisle seat in the row behind. I was reading the guide book I'd bought and turned round to ask Bob a question.

"How do you pronounce this flower festival place?" I asked him.

I'd tried to read the name from the guide book once or twice, trying the vowel sounds in different ways. The man sitting next to Bob answered when Bob told me he didn't know. He said that he was from Amsterdam and that the first word I'd tried was the closest to the way it should be pronounced.

"But when you get there," he continued, "you'll just pronounce it 'Wow!'"

I smiled and thanked him and told mum what the Dutchman had said. Although I didn't know what plants I'd be looking at, I was feeling quite excited about getting there and exploring fields and parks filled with flowers. If only mum and Bob would get along when we were there … but I wasn't going to hold my breath.

After we'd landed and unpacked at the hotel, Bob had to meet the supplier who'd gifted us our Holland mini-break. Mum and I did some sight-seeing and had dinner in a cosy, traditional restaurant across the road from our hotel.

We were to be picked up by coach from the hotel the next morning for our visit to the tulip fields and the flower festival with the unpronounceable name. Mum and I kissed goodnight and arranged to meet up for breakfast nice and early the next day.

That night, by the time Bob came back from his meeting with the bulb supplier who had wined and dined him in true Dutch hospitality style, I was in bed half-asleep. I was
feeling slightly queasy but didn't say anything to Bob, thinking I'd be fine in the morning. But the next day, I woke with one of the worst migraines I had ever suffered and I still felt very queasy too. Mum said she felt fine so I ruled out feeling poorly from the food from the night before as we'd eaten the same chicken casserole. But I also knew there'd be no way I'd be able to enjoy the day ahead. I insisted that Bob and mum went on the coach trip without me.

"I'm not leaving you in this state," said Bob. "We'll cancel, we can come back another time."
"Go, Bob. Just go, please. I think I just need to sleep this off and have some peace and quiet. I don't think I'm up to walking around all day. And mum's been looking forward to it so much…"
Bob groaned.

"Oh, you don't have to entertain her, just talk to her, for heaven's sake." I said, exasperated. "Just keep an eye on her, will you? Now … go!"

Left alone in my hotel room, I switched on the television and propped myself up in the bed against one of the deep, plump pillows. From the room I could hear the coach pull up outside of the hotel to collect mum and Bob. I peeked out of the window and watched as they both boarded the coach. A smile spread over my face as I watched the tour guide position them in seats next to each other. There was no way Bob could sit in the row behind mum today!

I glanced at the room service menu and picked out a light lunch I would treat myself to if I kept on feeling better during the day. I thought about Bob and mum traveling together, in silence - once their concern for me had been discussed, I hoped.

As I kept on feeling brighter I ran a deep bath in the swish en-suite bathroom. This, I imagined, would have been about the time the coach arrived at the tulip fields. Bob would have been making notes of the locations and suppliers, and mum would have been photographing windmills in fields striped with reds, yellows and whites.

By the time my bath bubbled up with some of the hotel's luxury toiletries I'd thrown in, the two of them would have been treated to Dutch cheese and wine at one of the stops the coach made that day.

And as I eased myself out of the scented water and relaxed on the bed in a white fluffy gown, that's when Bob and mum had their first proper conversation. They'd arrived at the flower festival and both had been stunned by its beauty. The park was a showcase of more than seven million bulbs, all in bloom at the very same time.

"It says here on this leaflet there are over 800 varieties of tulips!" Bob exclaimed as they walked into the park. "And 32 hectares of flowers!"
"Well, let's not waste any time, we've got a lot to see," mum smiled, and with that the two of them were off, together, on a mission to photograph and catalogue as many as they possibly could. They pointed out tulips to each other that they both admired, and read up about rare specimens they'd never seen before. The whole park was a kaleidoscope of colour of every kind of tulip, daffodil and hyacinth they'd ever seen before, and some they never knew existed. They drank it all in for the remainder of the morning.

By the time they had paused for lunch in the park I was up and dressed and walking out of the hotel to the pharmacy that I'd spotted the night before. Fortunately the shop assistant spoke perfect English and she helped me find what I needed, making sure that the instructions inside were printed in English too. I had a feeling I knew what was making me so queasy and back in the hotel room, the pregnancy test kit confirmed it.

When mum and Bob returned from their day out, Bob's face was flushed from the soft spring sunshine. He talked non-stop about their visit, calling it the ultimate theme park for gardeners. When he took a shower before dinner, he sang, something I'd not heard him do for a very long time. After he'd freshened up and had found his own white fluffy gown that the hotel had provided, he walked back into the bedroom, still full of news about his day at the park. I could hardly get a word in but if I didn't tell him our baby news soon I knew I would burst.

Later, I suggested to Bob that we ring mum to tell her that we'd join her in the hotel restaurant for dinner.
"I'll do it," he said.
I sat, open-mouthed and watched as Bob rang mum from his phone. Oh, I couldn't have been happier. Bob winked at me as he talked to mum on the phone. "And we've got some news to share with you too," he told mum at the end of the call. "Ok, then … yes … we'll see you about seven."

As we were leaving the room to head downstairs to eat, Bob hesitated.
"Hold on a minute," he said: "There's something I want to give to your mum."
He opened his backpack that he'd taken with him on the coach and pulled out a small blue plastic bag covered with the logo of the park that they'd been to that day.
"Tulip bulbs," he told me. "It's a variety called 'Friendship' … your mum admired them today in the park so I thought I'd buy some bulbs for her. Do you think she'd mind if I offered to plant them for her at home?"

As I've said, I don't know much about flowers and plants, but this is one variety that I hope will take root, grow strongly and flower beautifully too.

The Little Italian Coffee Shop

Carina sank into a chair by the window of her coffee shop and stared out at the rain on the street. A few moments later, her husband Mark joined her, taking a seat on the opposite side of the small window table. "The news is as bad as we feared," Carina said, sliding the letter across the formica table top to Mark. He scanned the sheet of paper in front of him, taking in its official council logo at the top. His shoulders dropped as he read down the letter and that's when Carina knew he'd reached the three dreaded words that they'd been in fear of receiving for so long… Compulsory Purchase Order.

"Nothing we can do about it now," Mark sighed.
"We did our best love," Carina said. "We did all that we could."
"Over 400 people signed our petition though!" Mark cried and Carina saw his eyes misting over. "All those people, our customers, our friends, some of them have been coming here for years, decades even. We've got generations of families who love this place, they were all behind us, all wanting to keep Freddy's Café open. And now this…" he picked up the letter again and shook it angrily. "It's all come to nothing, hasn't it?"
"We can start again, Mark," Carina said gently, although she was less sure in her heart about what they would do. "Maybe we can buy a coffee shop franchise this time, make it a bit easier on ourselves. There are new coffee shops opening all over town these days. We can…"
"… no Carina, we can't," said Mark, shaking his head.

Both of them felt defeated after months of wrangling with the council over their plans to buy up the street on which their coffee shop stood. It had first opened in the 1940s when Carina's grandfather Alfredo arrived from Italy to start a new life. And when he arrived in wet and cold England from the sunshine of Sorrento he decided to open up his own Italian coffee shop. Customers flocked from far and wide to visit the little Italian coffee shop with its space-age coffee machine hissing and spluttering and steaming away behind the counter. When Alfredo installed the machine that he imported from Italy, it developed a tic, letting out a gentle hiss of steam when it thought no-one was looking. But the machine not only lasted through Alfredo's years when he ran the café, it lasted through his son Gianfranco's reign too. And then the café had been passed down to Carina who had run it with her husband Mark for over ten years. Alfredo's coffee machine was still put to good use, a genuine piece of Italy, working right there in their café. And it still to this day, without fail, let out an unexpected gentle hiss of steam now and then.

"It's there in black and white, Mark," Carina said, pointing at the letter. "We have no choice, we have to move on. The council are selling the land to build new houses and we're the last of the shops on the street to be forced out. We knew it was coming, Mark. It's our turn and we have to go too."

Carina tried her best to sound stronger than she felt. She knew that to lose the business wouldn't mean the end of the world to them both as they were still young, and brave enough to start again. She didn't relish the thought of taking on a bland coffee shop franchise in town but they both knew the business and could make it work. It was the loss of Freddy's Café itself that Carina would mourn, her whole history was here in this place. They'd tried everything to save it. They'd formally objected to the council plans and had attended meetings at the council. And when none of that seemed to work, one of their customers started a petition which had over 400 signatures on it by the time Carina and Mark handed it in at their Town Hall. But the council had already made their decision. Dave Hall, their local MP, had done all he could to help too.

"I'll miss the place as much as anyone," he'd told Carina. "I remember happy times spent in here as a boy, eating ice-cream floats served by your father Gianfranco behind the counter. He always wore a funny little white hat and his striped apron, and oh, Carina, the best ice-cream and pastries he would serve!"

But memories counted for nothing where business was concerned, Carina knew, and the compulsory purchase order had finally landed on their doormat that morning.

Carina looked around Freddy's Café, the place that had been part of her life for as long as she could remember. Her first job working there was on Saturday afternoons, helping her grandparents fold napkins and polish the spoons. Then when she was older, she worked during the week after school helping her parents to clear up at the end of another busy day.

"We could sell off some of the furniture," Mark suggested, watching Carina, but she shook her head. "Who'd want this old stuff?" she said. "All the dark wooden units that grandad brought from Italy once the café started to make a bit of money. The drawers under the counter are heavier than they look - and as for those stools along the counter, they went out of fashion decades ago." Carina ran her hand across the table top. "And I'm not sure this colour of formica ever came into fashion either."

Mark reached out to hold Carina's hand. He remembered the day he first met her here in the café. He'd only called into Freddy's Café to escape the rain outside. He'd ordered a cappuccino from the girl behind the counter who was wearing a little white hat and a striped apron. He knew how much this place meant to her, how much it meant to them both.

"And that coffee machine's an antique," Mark said. "We might be able to get something for it at auction." "That old thing?" Carina said in surprise. "It's been on its last legs for years."

And as if to make the point, a gentle hiss of steam escaped from the coffee machine, which made Carina and Mark smile at each other for the first time that day.

Once Carina flipped the café door sign to OPEN the day went by in a blur. Without exception, the customers who called in were upset about the news, disappointed to hear that their favourite coffee shop was set to close.

"Where will I go for my espresso now?" asked Jim who liked to spend weekday mornings sitting in his favourite seat reading his newspaper and keeping an eye on the world through the coffee shop window. All day, Carina served behind the counter, trying to keep a smile on her face. Mark worked the temperamental coffee machine and rang sales into the old Italian cash register that Alfredo once owned. Behind the counter, framed photographs of Alfredo and Gianfranco with their families looked down from the walls into the cosy café space below.   When their local MP came into the coffee shop later that day, Carina's smile finally dropped. As much as Dave Hall had helped to fight with them to keep the shop open, she really didn't want to have anything to do with anyone from the council, not today of all days.

"I'm very sorry, Carina," Dave said, as he bought a cappuccino and took a seat at one of the tables. She watched as the MP opened up a small laptop and placed it on the table. Carina busied herself restocking the cups and saucers while behind her the coffee machine hissed its disapproval, as if it knew exactly what was going on.

"Carina?" she heard. "Have you got a minute?"

She turned to see Dave standing at his table, beckoning her to go to him. She dried her hands on a tea towel, straightened her apron, pushed a loose strand of her dark hair behind one ear and walked over towards him.

"Here, look at this," he said, turning the laptop towards her.

Carina scanned the web page that Dave had opened up. It was a news item about heritage funding that had been given to a living museum. Dave pointed to the screen.

"It says here they've been given funding to invest in a vintage coffee shop," Dave said, his eyes gleaming.

Carina shook her head, confused.

"A 1940s coffee shop," Dave continued.

"But, what on earth does it mean?" asked Carina, taking a seat beside Dave.

"Well, these living museums.." said Dave, "...I've seen it done before, they want to be as authentic as possible, so instead of building a new coffee shop and making it look old, they prefer to buy one and move it, brick by brick."

Carina's eyes widened.

"I've seen it done a few times before," Dave continued. "The museum's already bought an ice-cream parlour and moved it to their 1960s outdoor section. And they're in the process of moving an old police station too. Every seat, every brick, every wall tile, every light fitting is taken out and moved and reconstructed on the museum site."

"And you think the museum will be interested in this place?" she asked, astonished.

"There's no harm in putting in a proposal," Dave said, stroking his chin. "Leave it with me and I'll see what I can do. Something as unique as this place deserves to be saved, it's what I've always said."

-0-

At the grand opening of Freddy's Café in the grounds of the living museum, the Mayor gave a speech and the Lady Mayoress cut a ribbon in the colours of the Italian flag. The façade of the café was new, created from drawings and plans by the museum staff but the inside of the café was Alfredo's original, if a little smaller than it once used to be. The dark wooden counter was in its rightful place with the stools lined up in front. The formica tables and chairs were ready and waiting for their first customers. TV reporters filmed Carina and Mark who talked about their donation of the café fixtures and fittings to the living museum.

The museum manager stood politely to one side to allow Carina to talk to the press who had come to write about the Italian café. Finally when Carina had a moment to herself, the museum manager took her to one side and offered her the job of running the café. "That's if you'd like to, of course," he told her. "And you could train our volunteers to use the antique coffee machine. They don't seem able to get it to work as well as you."

Carina smiled broadly at the offer and glanced across at a line of customers waiting to enter the museum café. Old Jim was first in line, ready to try an espresso and sit at his favourite seat to read his newspaper and look out now onto a different world from the window.

And at the end of the day, when all of the guests had gone home and the café was quiet once more, Carina and Mark headed towards the exit, leaving Freddy's Café in the safe hands of the museum staff. It was no longer theirs to own, but there was no doubt that Carina's grandfather's legacy would live on for others to enjoy. After one last glance around the place, Carina ran her hand along the warm counter top. She turned to Mark and smiled. They left, and as they closed the door behind them, Alfredo's coffee machine let out a soft and gentle hiss.

The New Man

"Oh, a pie!" Jeff did his best to keep a smile on his face. "How thoughtful of you. But really, you shouldn't have."

Bev Jenkins handed over the meat and potato pie she'd placed on her finest plate and wrapped in her best tea-towel.

"It's nothing," she said. "Just a little gift, to say welcome to the neighbourhood."

"Well, that's very kind of you," he said.

Bev did her best to peer past Jeff, trying to get a glimpse into the hallway of his new home, but Jeff wasn't budging.

"Well, thanks again," he nodded. "I'm Jeff. Sorry, but I don't know your name?"

"I'm Bev. I live down at number four. So if you're ever passing or you need anything..." she winked "... anything at all, well, you know where I am."

Bev smiled brightly and hopefully, but Jeff chose not to respond.

"I'm sure this pie will be delicious," he said. "But I'm really sorry, Bev, I hope you'll excuse me. I'm in the middle of stripping wallpaper and I really must crack on."

"Maybe I could pop by tomorrow and help?" Bev asked, a little too keenly for Jeff's liking. "And I'm a dab-hand in the garden, I could help sort out your borders for you, mow the lawn, that sort of thing?"

"Thanks Bev. It's very kind of you, but I think I'm all right for now. I'll give you a shout if I need anything. Number four, you say?"

"Yes, that's right. The one with the red front door. My sister Lynn lives next door at number six."

"Lynn?" Jeff asked, surprised. "Oh, I think I might have met her already."

Bev's face clouded over and she turned to walk away. "I'll be seeing you then," she said as she walked down the garden path.

Jeff closed the front door after Bev left and headed into the kitchen with the plate pie in his hand. When he reached the kitchen he opened the fridge door and placed the pie on the shelf, right next to the pie he'd received earlier that day, from the woman he now knew was Bev's sister, Lynn.

Later that evening, Jeff rang his sister, who wanted to hear all the news about his new house and the neighbours.

"Oh, the neighbours!" he laughed. "I only moved in yesterday and I've already had two women round this morning to welcome me - and both of them brought gifts."

"Gifts?" asked Louise. "What sort of gifts?"

"Pies! One's meat and potato and I'm not entirely sure what's in the other one!"

"Oh Jeff, and you don't even like pastry, do you?" she laughed.

"Lou, I hadn't the heart to decline either of them," he said. "They were nice women, both of them, if not a little…" Jeff reached to find the right word. "…they weren't exactly desperate but they were more than a little keen, if you take my meaning. A bit too pushy, perhaps."

"Sounds to me like you're going to be a bit of a catch now you're single again, bruv."

"To be honest, Lou, I just want some peace and quiet, you know? I'd quite like some time on my own, just till I find my feet again."

"I know Jeff. Divorce is never easy and you've been through the mill these last few months. I do understand, you know. And you're not entirely on your own, you've got little Bobby to keep you company."

Jeff looked down at his little terrier, lying on the floor at his feet, softly snoring.

"Well at least I managed to hang on to something from the wreck of our marriage," he said. "I'm still surprised she didn't press her solicitor to get Bobby, she managed to get her hands on just about everything else I ever had."

"Oh now, come on Jeff. Don't start going over all that again. It's time to move on. You're still a young man, and you're having a fresh start in a new house in a new town."

"Thanks Lou, you're right. I'll let you know when I've got the spare room ready and you and Tom can bring the boys over one weekend, eh?"

"That'd be great. I'll speak to you soon, Jeff and I hope you settle in all right. Oh, one thing before I go…"

"Yes, Lou?"

"What on earth are you going to do with those pies?"

"It's not the pies I'm worried about," Jeff laughed. "It's those two sisters!"

The next morning, Lynn Jenkins closed her front door behind her and headed out down her garden path to the top of Rose Avenue. When Bev heard her sister's front door slam, she too set off from her house at number four and headed out onto their street. The two sisters huffed in pretend surprise when they caught sight of each other walking in the same direction.

"I'm only calling in on him to get my plate and tea-towel back, you know," Bev said.

"And I'm just popping in to see if he needs any help wall-papering," Lynn sniffed.

"You look a bit overdressed to be going wall-papering," Bev said, noticing her sister's tight black jeans and high heels. "And you've had something done to your hair."

Lynn didn't reply, she just picked up her pace so that Bev had to trot behind her to catch up. And it wasn't easy to trot, not in the new wedge heel shoes Bev had bought specially to try to impress her new neighbour. When the sisters reached Jeff's garden gate, there was a tussle to see which of them could get through it first. As usual, Lynn won and Bev followed her older sister to the front door. It was Lynn's knock at the door that Jeff heard as he was painting the kitchen skirting boards. He was just about to put the paintbrush down and answer the door when he heard what sounded like two women bickering.

"I saw him first, you know. So by rights you shouldn't even be here!"

"Just because you're older than me doesn't mean you always get first dibs on everything - and everyone - you know!"

Jeff stood stock-still in the kitchen, hardly breathing, as if his tiniest movements might give the game away and announce his presence. Lynn knocked again and when there was no reply, the sisters finally turned, chatting to each other as they walked away.

"I might pop back this afternoon," Lynn said. "If I've nothing better to do, of course."

"You've never got anything better to do," Bev replied. "All you ever do is keep an eye open, ready to pounce on new fellas in the village."

"I beg your pardon?" Lynn exploded. "You're no better! And I do have other things going on in my life you know."

"Such as?"

"Such as… cooking and baking. I cooked that pie for him yesterday."

"You did not! I saw the supermarket box in your bin!"

"And I suppose you cooked your pie from scratch did you?"

Bev hesitated before she replied. "How else would I have done it?"

"A little birdie told me you bought it at the bakery yesterday morning," Lynn said. "Just like you bought that birthday cake once, remember? You were 14 years old and you told mum you'd baked her a cake and I know for a fact that you bought it at the bakery. That Joe lad who used to fancy me, he told me you'd bought it there and you passed it off as your own to our very own mother!".

"Joe from the bakery? Oh, drag him up, why don't you? And he never fancied you! He fancied me!"

And with that, the bickering sisters walked back to their houses at number four and number six, leaving Jeff breathing a sigh of relief at number twenty-two.

In need of a breather and some fresh air while the paint dried, Jeff decided to take the dog for a walk around their new neighbourhood. He packed a few things into his rucksack, slung it over one shoulder and headed out to explore the village that was now his home.

"That's a lovely little dog. What's his name?"

"Bobby," smiled Jeff. The woman stroked the dog's face and scratched behind its ears. In return, Bobby rolled over, expecting a tummy rub - and he wasn't disappointed.

"I'm Eleanor," she said, offering her hand to Jeff. She looked around her in the park. "And my dog's called Sammy, he's around here somewhere. I just let him off the lead and he has a run around the park but always comes back to this bench. He knows I'll be here, I always like to sit and read in this spot when the weather's nice. Oh! Here he is!" she said, pointing. Jeff turned and saw a large chocolate coloured dog bounding towards them. He gathered Bobby to him, anxious that the terrier might be frightened of the larger, more boisterous dog. But he needn't have worried, the two of them seemed to take an instant liking to each other.

"Have you had Sammy very long?" asked Jeff.

"Just a few months," Eleanor replied. "He came from a rescue shelter. I got him after I... well, I was at a stage in my life when I wanted a little bit of company that wasn't another person, if you know what I mean."

Jeff's forehead wrinkled. He didn't want to seem rude and pry.

"What I mean is, I'd just got divorced and I was rattling around in a house after my husband left, so I decided to get a dog to keep me company. I know, it sounds a bit daft."

"No, it doesn't," Jeff smiled. "I understand completely. I'm in a similar boat myself. My divorce has just been finalised and now it's just me and little Bobby here. We're both having a new start."

Eleanor suddenly cried out and scolded her dog. "Sammy! Don't do that!" Jeff turned to see what was happening and caught the big dog with its nose inside his rucksack.

"Come away from there, Sammy. Leave it," Eleanor said. She turned to Jeff. "I'm so sorry. He must be attracted to something inside."

She gently pulled Sammy away from Jeff's bag and the dog stood politely at Eleanor's side with his tail wagging furiously.

Jeff opened the rucksack and lifted out something that was covered tightly with a plastic bag. Sammy's tail wagged even harder. Even Bobby was interested, trying to jump up onto Jeff's knee to see what was going on and where the smell was coming from.

Jeff slid the contents out of the plastic bag. Eleanor tried to stifle a giggle when she saw the plate pie in Jeff's hands.

"I'm not sure what to do with it," he said, smiling. "I can't eat pastry, it's never agreed with me and I've been given it as a gift. It's meat and potato, I think," he said, poking the crust with a finger.

"I think Sammy and Bobby might like a little bite," Eleanor suggested. Jeff broke off a couple of chunks and placed them on the ground. The dogs gulped down the pie and Jeff found himself laughing at the absurdity of it all. His laughter made Eleanor giggle too.

"I don't suppose you'd like to meet up again tomorrow, would you?" she asked. "It's not a date or anything. Just the four of us, here on this bench, tomorrow afternoon and we'll go for a walk around the park?"

"That sounds lovely," said Jeff. "Same time? Same place?"

Eleanor nodded.

"And it's not a date?" he smiled.

"It's definitely not a date!" she laughed.

"Then I think I can handle that," said Jeff. "And I just might have another pie I can bring!"

The Rock and Roll Headmistress

From the very first moment Sue Connor took to the stage to address her staff and pupils, it was clear that life at St. George's school was never going to be quite the same again.

The staff had already met Sue, but this was the first time the pupils had been called to an assembly given by their new headmistress. It was hard to know how they were going to react to a new head coming in. Robert Hughes, who had just retired, had worked at the school for over 30 years and had been very much loved by all at the school and in the town too. Robert had worked at St. George's so long that he'd taught parents of most of the pupils, and in some cases, their grandparents too. But now he'd retired as headmaster and the feeling was that he would definitely be missed. From the teaching staff and the pupils through to the caretakers and the kitchen staff, everyone held Robert Hughes in high regard and friendship. He had a warm and friendly style, engaging and interacting with everyone that he met. Under his leadership, St George's school had won awards for academic excellence. And in his tenure as the leader of the school, Robert Hughes had come to represent everything that an excellent headmaster should be.

"He's been so good with the children," Pete Brown, the PE teacher said in the staff room earlier that morning. "I doubt we'll see the likes of him again."
"His replacement's going to take a bit of getting used to," said Bev Smith, the maths tutor. "What's her name again… Susan Connor, isn't it?"

"I'm sure her name rings a bell," said Pete. He started puzzling over how and why he recognised it and mulled her name over again. "Connor… Susan Connor."

"Well, we'll see her in full force at the assembly. She's going to introduce herself to the pupils." Bev looked at her watch. "Come on, we'd better go, we don't want to be late to the first assembly given by our new boss."

All eyes were on Sue Connor as she walked to the podium in the middle of the stage to give her welcome speech to the school. Pete and Bev stood at the back of the hall along with the other staff, intrigued to see how their new head would perform.

From the very first moment she stood from her seat at one side of the stage, Sue Connor commanded the stage with her presence and style. Her outfit, chosen carefully to wear on the first day in her new job, was a cerise trouser suit with a black polo neck sweater and she was as neat as a pin. But there was something else about her, something more. Bev tried to define it, as she watched her new boss take to the stage. There was something about Sue Connor that suggested there was more fun bursting to be released from her soul than could be allowed in her work situation. And those shoes, Bev noticed, what wonderful, funky black stilettos she wore.

With her long, thick black hair, her suit cinched in to emphasis her waist and legs that went on forever, it's fair to say that Sue's arrival caused quite a stir. Two of the sixth form boys nudged each other and one of them gave a low whistle, for which he received a hard stare from Mr Duke, who taught French. It was a stare which threatened that Mr Duke would be speaking in harsh tones to the sixth form boy later on.

At the assembly, Sue's speech was friendly, warm and perfectly pitched. Her words were stirring, powerful and emotional as she paid homage to Robert Hughes and promised to build on the legacy of his work at the school.

When the assembly finished, Bev whispered to Peter: "That was quite a performance!" And from the round of applause the pupils gave at the end of the speech, it was clear that the rest of the school agreed. The applause was almost as enthusiastic and noisy as it had been for the leaving speech from Robert Hughes. It was clear, that with the pupils at least, Sue Connor was a hit.
"Performance?" said Pete. "Oh, yes, I agree," and again, a memory stirred within him. He felt as if he had seen Sue Connor somewhere before – but where?

In her role as the new head of St George's, one of the first things that Sue Connor did was to encourage the pupils to become more involved in drama, music and dance. Sue Connor was an advocate of the arts and she implemented new, more creative and ambitious after-school clubs.

A school musical was planned, a rock opera, to take place on the last day of term. It would be a show that friends and families would be invited to attend. Mike Harvey, the drama teacher, loved Sue's idea and set to work on production in his new drama club. The musical stirred up a real buzz around the school. Rehearsals began and there were rumours flying around about who would be in it, playing which parts and singing which songs.

In the staff room one lunchtime, Pete Brown sidled over to Bev for a quiet word. He held his phone in his hand.

"I knew there was something familiar about our new boss," he whispered excitedly.

"Who? Sue Connor?"

"The very one. Or should I say, Sue Connor of Sue Connor and the Connorellos!"

Bev raised her eyebrows. "You've lost me, Pete."

"Look!" Peter showed his phone to Bev. It was open on an internet page and on the screen stood a girl with dark bobbed hair. She was wearing a leather jumpsuit, hands on her hips, staring straight into the camera, as if she was daring the photographer to take her picture. Bev stared at the picture long and hard.

"It can't be her, can it?" Bev asked, but she knew it must be. The resemblance was too strong.

"I knew I'd seen her somewhere before," Pete said. "The Connorellos were a pop band in the eighties. They were very low key but they did have a hit that made it into the charts. *Send me Sweetness* it was called. The song was a one-hit wonder but the band made it onto TV a couple of times, just local programmes, I remember. And they played some gigs in town too. Sue was the lead singer."

"Well, fancy that," said Bev. "We've got our very own rock and roll headmistress!" she laughed.

"At least it helps to explain why she's so keen on getting the kids fired up about the musical," said Pete.

"It also helps to explain those amazing black shoes," thought Bev.

"What are you two giggling about?" a voice behind them said gently. Bev gulped when she saw who it was and hoped that Sue Connor hadn't been able to hear anything they'd said.

"We're just saying how great the musical's going to be at the end of term show."

"I have to admit that music's a passion of mine," said Sue. "It always has been. And in all the years I've been teaching I've kept myself involved in performance, mainly local theatre. I love all that sort of thing, you know, amateur dramatics and performing in my spare time."

"Well, we had heard…" said Sue shyly, glancing over at Pete. But Pete had been collared by Dennis Duke and the two of them were deep in conversation with Pete showing Dennis the picture of a young Sue Connor on his phone.

"Oh, really? What have you heard, I wonder?" asked Sue with a smile in her voice.

Bev didn't want to lie to Sue but she also didn't want to land Pete in hot water with the new boss.

"We heard that you were a singer yourself," Bev said hesitantly. "Back in the day. I mean. At least, that's what we heard."

Sue laughed. "Well, it didn't take long for that cat to be let out of the bag, did it? It was a very long time ago." Sue winked at Bev. "Mind you, it was fun while it lasted. My husband and I had some real adventures. He was the drummer in the band in his spare time. He worked for the local paper as a photographer and took the publicity shots of the band to send out to agents. I remember there was one particular picture he took of me when I was, oh, I must have been early twenties, and I was dressed up in a leather catsuit. Can you imagine?"

Bev could easily imagine, having just seen the picture on Pete's phone. Sue Connor had been a knock-out back in the day and she was still very stylish now. Just then, Sue's attention was caught by the drama teacher who had entered the room.

"Sorry, Beverley. I just need to go and have a word with Mike Harvey," said Sue. "There's something I'd like to speak to him about involving the musical. It's a mad idea but it might just work, especially if everyone now knows about the Connorellos."

When the end of term show was staged, it was standing room only in the assembly hall. Families and friends of the pupils filled every row and extra seats had to be brought in from the classrooms. The show was a resounding success with all of the pupils' hard work paying off. The pupils had done it all, from writing the script and playing instruments, creating and designing scenes and props to acting and singing in the show. Parents and family members were very proud indeed. Even Robert Hughes returned to the school to be part of the audience watching the show he'd been hearing so much about over the last few weeks.

When the applause finally died down at the end of the show, Sue Connor took to the stage and gave thanks to everyone involved. As it was the last day of term before the summer holidays, her speech drew on how encouraged she had been by all the hard work and how she had been inspired to produce another show like it again next year.

"I have one final thing I'd like to say to you all before you leave for the holidays," Sue said, and the audience waited to hear what her announcement would be. Sue slipped out of her formal work jacket and placed it over a chair at the side of the stage. Then, she grabbed the microphone and looked over to the school orchestra where Mike Harvey was poised with his baton raised.

"Hit it, guys!" she yelled.

The school orchestra started up and the introduction to an old, familiar tune started to play. As the first bars of the music worked its magic on the audience, she unpinned her hair and shook it loose over her shoulders. Excitement rippled around the hall. In the audience, Paul Johnson's dad turned to his son and embarrassed him to bits, saying: "Do you know son, I used to have Sue Connor's poster on my wall when I was a lad."

Sue smiled out to the audience.

"It's been more years than I care to remember since I last sang in public," she announced.

"But here we go! If you know the words, join in and sing along!"

The audience went wild, cheering and clapping, the excitement of the last day of term building up to a wild finale.

"Happy holidays, everyone," the headmistress announced to the hall when the applause finally died down.
"Have a great summer – and we'll see you next term!"
In the audience, Robert Hughes was first to get up and out of his seat, leading a standing ovation to the new head.

The Ruby Heart

"Mr and Mrs Ward?" the receptionist called. "You can come through now."

The young woman stood from behind her reception desk and beckoned Marie and Dave to follow.

Marie took hold of her husband's hand.

"Are you ready?" she whispered.

Dave took a deep breath. "I'm ready," he replied.

The couple followed the receptionist along a carpeted hallway into a well-lit room that overlooked a small garden.

"This is Michael," the receptionist said. "I'll leave you both in his capable and experienced hands."

A smiling young man with a thick black beard shook Marie's hand.

"I expect we're some of your oldest customers," Dave laughed nervously.

"Not at all," said Michael. "We get all ages in here. You'd be surprised!"

It was much later when Marie and Dave finished their business with Michael.

"Fancy a cuppa now it's over?" Marie smiled with relief.

"Not half," Dave replied. "We can pop across the road to the tea-room in the hospital and see your friend Jean. She might be serving today."

"Good idea," said Marie.

"Have you heard from mum today?" Claire asked her sister.

"No," Karen replied. "Actually, come to think of it, she didn't ring yesterday either."

"Do you think she's all right?" Claire said.

"Mum? Course she's all right. What are you worrying for?"

"Dad hasn't said anything to you, has he?" Claire asked.

"No…" replied Karen. "But come to think about it, he's been acting a bit strange lately, have you noticed? Sort of secretive."

"I rang them both yesterday and again this morning and there's been no answer."

"Oh…" said Karen. "Then I think we should call round and see them."

"I've just been round," said Claire. "And they weren't in."

"But they're always in!" cried Karen. "Where could they have gone?"

"That's what I'm trying to tell you, I think there's something wrong with one of them."

"What do you mean? Mum's as fit as a fiddle, isn't she? And apart from his hip, dad's doing well."

"Well, I wasn't going to tell you this over the phone," said Claire. "But mum's friend Jean told me she saw them both at the hospital today. And mum's not said anything about a hospital appointment, has she said anything to you?"

"Nothing," said Karen, trying to mask the concern in her voice. "We'll have to keep ringing for the rest of today until one of them picks up. And if they don't, well, we'll have to go round and see them to find out what on earth's going on!"

Later that afternoon, Karen and Claire were waiting on the sofa in their old family home for their mum and dad to return.

Karen checked her watch for the umpteenth time.

"I wonder where they've gone?" sighed Claire. "They wouldn't be doing anything daft, would they?"

"Mum and dad?" cried Karen. "They've never done anything daft in their lives."

Just then, the sound of a car engine on the road outside made Karen jump up from the sofa. She looked out of the window.

"They're here! Claire!"

Claire ran to the front door and yanked it open as Marie and Dave pulled the car onto the drive. The two sisters stood to attention, one either side of the front door, waiting with arms crossed for their parents to explain themselves.

When Marie saw them both from the passenger seat of the car, she just smiled.

"You'll be wanting an explanation, I know. I know," Marie said as she got out of the car and walked towards the house. "Come on through to the kitchen and I'll put the kettle on."

Dave followed the three women into the kitchen. When they were all together, Karen went to hug her mum but Marie backed away from her daughter.

"No hugging…" Marie winced. "I'm still a little sore."

"Oh, my word!" Karen cried. "I knew it, it's bad news!"

"Dad?" Claire pleaded, but he too backed away as if shielding himself from his daughter's touch.

Karen sunk into one of the kitchen chairs around the big oak family table.

"It's all right mum," Karen said. "I know you've been trying to spare us the bad news, but we know all about it."

"You do?" asked Marie in surprise.

"Yes, we know about your hospital visit."

Marie glanced over at Dave. "I knew Jean wouldn't keep quiet," she said.

Dave simply shrugged.

"We know mum, it's all right," Claire chipped in.

"We know. And we're here for you, every step of the way. Whatever you need, we're here for you."

Claire looked at her dad. "For both of you."

Marie glanced towards Dave and she saw a smile play around her husband's lips.

"Well, whatever it is you think you know, you don't," Marie smiled at her daughters.

"Yes, it's true that I have been into the hospital. We both have, me and your dad. I expect Jean told you both that she'd seen us?"

The girls nodded in unison.

"Look, sit down, both of you," Marie said. "I've got something to show you…"

She began, gingerly, to remove her coat.

"Dave?" Marie said and the girls watched as their dad carefully and slowly took off his jacket too.

The girls didn't know where to look first as bare arms were revealed from under their parents' coats.

"We celebrate 40 years together next week," said Dave.

"What better way to celebrate?" agreed Marie.

They were lost for words as their parents displayed matching, ruby heart tattoos at the top of their left arms.

Tina the taxi driver

"Are you picking up little Lord Fauntleroy this morning?" Sue asked when she served me my bacon sandwich and mug of tea.

It was Sue's nickname for Kevin, the boy I was paid to collect every weekday from one of the big detached houses along the seafront.

"I'm actually a bit worried about him," I told Sue. "He used to be such a chatty, cheerful little lad, keeping me company in the taxi on our journey every morning. But since he went back to school after his mum died, he's hardly said a word."

I took my sandwich and tea from Sue and headed to an empty table. I glanced at my watch to confirm that I still had half an hour to enjoy my breakfast before going to pick up Kevin, my first fare of the day.

Once my breakfast was over, I headed out of Sue's café.

"Have a good day, Tina!" she called when she saw me leave. "Drive safely!"

As soon as I stepped outdoors the cold wind whipped around me and I pulled my coat tight. Once safely inside my cab I checked my appearance in the mirror. After I'd smoothed my hair and dabbed on a bit of lipstick, I checked in with Ted at base control and let him know I was starting my day's work. And at eight o'clock precisely, I pulled the cab alongside the kerb outside of one of the biggest houses on this side of town. Kevin came out of his front door with his rucksack thrown across one shoulder of a school blazer that always looked a bit to large for his skinny frame.

"Morning, Kevin!" I said cheerfully.

"Morning," he replied, eyes downcast, as he clambered into the back of the cab. He usually sat in the front but I don't mind where my passengers sit. When they sit in the back, it's an indication that they don't really want to chat, they just want to stare at their phones or take in the scenery. I looked in the rear-view mirror and saw Kevin sitting quietly, staring ahead.

"You all right, Kevin? I asked him.

"I've lost something," he said quietly. "Something mum gave me, before she…" he stopped himself from talking further. Then I saw him turn his head to look out of the window, his eyes filling with tears. "It's nothing really, just a little yellow badge she bought for me on holiday once."

For the rest of the journey to Kevin's school my attempts to engage him in any kind of conversation proved futile and so I left him to his thoughts. The roads were clear and it wasn't long before I was dropping him off outside the school gates.

"I'll pick you up at four," I told him, although there really was no need for me to remind him. I'd been picking him up at four for the past few months so we both knew the drill.

"Ted, this is car sixteen checking in. I've just dropped Kevin off at his school," I radioed into base.

"Right-o, Tina," replied Ted. "Could you make a pick up next from 23 Windsor Lane? That's close by where you are now. We've got a passenger by the name of Jenkins going to the Royal Hospital on Sands Street."

"Will do, Ted, thank you," I replied. I swung the car in the direction of Windsor Lane. I was fond of the houses on the Windsor estate, they were lovely old Victoria semis, full of character and with long front gardens too. I could only dream of being able to afford to live on the Windsor estate. My cabbie earnings combined with Jim's salary from the building society were just enough to keep us afloat as it was. But while we might not have been wealthy, we were happy, that's for sure. I knew I could never give up the freedom of driving my taxi.

I pulled up outside of number 23 where a woman was already waiting by the front door. It was only when she started walking down her garden path towards me that I realised she was heavily pregnant. I jumped out of my driving seat and walked around to help her in to the passenger side.

"You're going to the Royal Hospital, is that right?" I said as she settled into her seat, pulling the seatbelt to fit around her belly.

"To the ante natal unit, please, it's round the back of the old part of the hospital," she replied. "I've got an appointment this morning."

She continued tugging at the seat belt to try to get as much slack into it as possible so it would fit around her. In the end, I offered to help, I knew the little trick you had to pull with that seatbelt when it started acting up. Finally, she was safely plugged in and off we went, carefully and slowly pulling out of the Windsor estate into the traffic heading to town.

"When's your baby due?" I asked as we drove along.

"Oh, not for another week, the doctor reckons," she said. "But to be honest, I've been feeling a bit peculiar the last couple of days so the hospital said to pop in and get checked over. That's why I was waiting for you by the door there when you arrived in the cab, I couldn't seem to get comfortable sitting around in the house."

"Will you be all right sitting in the cab for the next five minutes before we reach the hospital?" I asked her, more than a little concerned.

"I'm sure I'll be fine," she said smiling, "if it's only five minutes or so… so… oh… OH… OH!"

"What is it?" I asked, alarmed. My mind started racing and my heart started pounding. I was driving along at 30 miles per hour with a pregnant woman – a heavily pregnant woman - in the passenger seat of my cab who'd turned red in the face and was sweating profusely!

"I think we need to get there in less than five minutes!" she panted, furiously breathing in and out of her mouth.

"I'm on it!" I cried and pressed my foot to the floor. I radioed to Ted, telling him to let the Royal Hospital know I was bringing in a heavily pregnant woman about to go into labour. With my deft manoeuvring the car sped to the hospital gates, through the grounds and straight to the doors of the maternity ward where a stretcher was waiting to whisk my passenger inside. With Mrs Jenkins safely inside the hospital, I drove off again.

"Did she pay you?" laughed Ted when I radioed in to let him know what had happened and that I was free to take another fare.

"Ted!" I chided. "I think we can put that fare down to experience – and I never want to go through anything like it again!"

"Got a nice quiet one for you now, Tina," he said. "It's an airport run for a passenger called Phil Smith. You're to pick him up near the roundabout for the motorway, his car's broken down and he needs to get the airport pretty sharp."

"Right-o, Ted. Car sixteen's on its way to the airport."

Phil Smith was easy to spot. He was the tall, harassed-looking fella standing beside his car in a lay-by. His car bonnet was propped open and steam gushed from underneath. As I pulled into the lay-by, I saw a pick-up truck follow and pull in after me. After consulting with the pick-up driver, Phil leaned into his car and took something from the glove box which he dropped into his jacket pocket. Then he jumped into the passenger seat of my cab, yanked the seatbelt around him and yelled. "Airport! Now! As quick as you can!"

"Looks like a nasty spot of bother with your car, there," I said by way of conversation. And for the next twenty minutes of our drive to the airport, Phil sighed and moaned about faulty pistons and gear boxes, engines and belts. Being a cabbie meant I knew every bit of my car inside and out and we chatted amicably until I was sure he'd calmed down enough for me to ask him what was really going on.

"Are you… off anywhere nice?" I asked him, knowing full well he hadn't put a suitcase or a bag in my cab.

"No," he smiled. "I'm meeting someone… my girlfriend actually. She's due back from a business trip and I said I'd pick her up when she landed but I'm really late now."

We approached the turn-off for the airport.

"Terminal 2?" I suggested and Phil nodded.

"Thanks, yes. And would you mind waiting while I go inside to collect her? And then take us back to my car, the pick-up truck driver said he'd have it fixed in no time."

I swung the cab into the waiting area for Terminal 2 and Phil leapt out of the passenger seat and ran into the terminal. I watched through the plate-glass windows as he ran to meet a dark-haired woman trailing a small wheeled suitcase behind her and I saw them embrace. Together they approached my car. I popped the suitcase in the boot and the couple sat close together on the back seat. My in-built sense of taxi diplomacy kicked in and I did my best to turn a blind eye to the canoodling going on in my cab. At the junction where I pulled off the motorway, Phil's voice piped up from the back seat.

"Would you mind if we stopped, just here? Just for a minute?"

I pulled the car over to the side of the road and Phil opened the car door. I watched as his tall frame unfolded from the back of the car and he knelt down on the roadside scrabbling in his pocket for something. In the rear-view mirror I watched as Phil, kneeling on the grass verge, asked his girlfriend to marry him.

And I saw his girlfriend, sitting on the back seat inside my cab, accept. I felt a warm rush to my throat and tears started to form behind my eyes, but knew I mustn't give in to them, not while I was driving and on duty at work. I drove on and when I finally dropped the couple off at the roundabout, Phil's car had been fixed. The tip that he handed over to me when he paid his fare showed just how much of a good mood he was in.

"Oh, and I found something in the back of the cab," Phil said after he paid his fare. "It must have fallen down the back of the seat." Phil handed over a tiny yellow badge with a sunshine face on it. "Mind you, it's probably nothing, looks just like a bit of old junk."

I tucked the badge away safely in my purse, looking forward to reuniting it with Kevin when I picked him up at four o'clock.

"Ted, this is car sixteen checking in. I'm taking a break and heading to Sue's café for coffee. I'll be free in thirty minutes when I'll check back in again."

"Thanks, Tina. Over and out!" said Ted.

I parked the car outside of Sue's café and walked inside.

"How's your morning been, Tina?" asked Sue as she made my coffee, just the way I like it and pouring it into my favourite mug.

"Oh, you know, nothing out of the ordinary - for a taxi driver, that is."

I opened my purse to pay Sue for the coffee.

"And how was little Lord Fauntleroy this morning?" she asked.

I glanced at the sunshine badge in my purse.

"It can't be easy for the lad, Sue," I told her. "But I have a feeling I'll be seeing his smile again soon."

Off to a Smashing Start

Diane knew she should have used a stronger box. But she'd been in such a hurry to pack up the last of her things from the old kitchen that she'd ended up piling everything into a tatty old cardboard box that had seen better days. As she walked up the path to the front door of her new home, Diane hugged the old box towards her. She was careful to carry it with both hands as it had started sagging at the bottom. But then she had to let one hand free, as she fumbled in her handbag looking for her door key. And with the other hand she tried, desperately, to stop the bottom of the box from ripping open any more than it already was.

With an awful sinking feeling, Diane felt the box inching out of her hands as its contents strained to escape. She tried, as quickly as she could, to unlock the front door. She pushed it wide open with her hip and managed to take one step inside the hall. And just as Diane took her first step into her new home, that's when the box slipped from her hands and her belongings scattered all over the floor.

She felt a hot rush of anger build up inside her. It wasn't quite the start to her new life she would have chosen. But she hadn't had much choice in moving out of the old house either, the home she'd shared with Mark, One night, after months of arguments and silent days between them, Mark finally admitted that he'd fallen in love with someone else. In the days that followed, the shock news sank in. Once the divorce papers were signed. Diane knew then she had to move out of the old house and start a new life.

She looked down at the hardwood floor where the mugs she'd brought to make coffee for the removal men were now smashed into shards. There was sugar spilled everywhere, mixed in with coffee and broken glass from the smashed coffee jar. Overwhelmed by the mess, it took a few moments for Diane to realise a dreadful whining noise was coming from inside the house.

"Oh no! The alarm!" she cried.

She stepped over the tattered box and broken glass, the coffee and the sugar, and headed along the hall to the alarm panel. She typed in the four-digit code that the estate agent had given her. She typed it in again, and again, but still the dreaded alarm sounded, piercing her eardrums.

"You all right in there?" a voice shouted across the din.

Diane turned to see a young woman, standing just outside of the open front door.

"I saw you come in, just now, and then I heard the alarm going off. Reckoned you must be our new neighbour. That alarm's always been a nuisance. I can show you how to switch it off, if you like?"

Diane smiled and breathed a sigh of relief.

"Yes, please do," she said, standing back to allow the woman access to the panel. It was switched off in seconds, as if it was the easiest thing in the world.

"Oh, sorry…" she said, extending her hand. "I'm Susan, from next door, number 37."

"I'm Diane, nice to meet you." Diane pointed to the alarm panel. "And thank you, for your help there."

"We've been looking forward to you moving in. There hasn't been anyone living in here for a few months since the last owner moved to Spain. My husband Rob and I, we used to keep the house keys for the owner and look after the place for them, that's how I know the alarm is temperamental," she explained. "Is your family moving in too?"

Diane shook her head.

"No, it's just me. I'm… well, I suppose you could say I'm downsizing. And the first thing I need to do after cleaning up that glass in the hallway is learn how to use this flaming alarm. Guess I'm going to have to get used to doing things on my own, now."

"Well if you need help settling in, I'm just next door. I can show you how to reset the alarm code too, when you're ready. Nice to meet you, Diane." And with that she was gone, leaving Diane on her own once again. She closed the front door and stood in the silence of the hallway. She closed her eyes and breathed in the unfamiliar air of a house that would become her new home. Then she bent down and gingerly started moving the broken glass and shards from the mugs. They could be thrown away, they were things she could replace. It was her shattered life that was in need of repair.

The removal van came and went with a minimum of fuss. A well-organised team of lifters and shifters brought her furniture in and positioned it for her. And after they left, Diane was surrounded by familiar objects from her old life with Mark.

A framed picture they'd bought on honeymoon now stood in bubble-wrap on her living room floor. A toaster that had once warmed four slices for their breakfast treats of eggs with smoked salmon now poked from the top of a box labelled 'Kitchen'.

"Come on, Diane!" she told herself. "You can do this. You can!"

She started with the box labelled 'Bedroom' and took out a duvet and bedding to make up her new bed.

"I haven't seen this in a while," she thought, as she shook out a duvet cover with a pretty daisy print. It was one she had made herself, each stitch crafted with the sewing machine that she'd treated herself to. She ran her hands across the dainty floral print, remembering that Mark had never liked it, and so it had sat, unused, at the bottom of their airing cupboard for years. The empty double bed stared back at Diane after she'd made it all up. She still wasn't used to sleeping on her own, not after years with Mark.

"But at least it looks pretty," she thought. "And it's all mine."

That night, exhausted after a busy day unpacking, Diane slept more soundly than she thought she would. The stress of the previous day's moving had taken its toll. And when she woke, under the daisy print duvet, it was with a sense of adventure in her heart.

She lay still for a while, cherishing the sound of the birds outside her bedroom window, welcoming her into the new day. She ran through the chores she had to do in the day ahead, starting with buying new mugs, coffee and checking out the local shops. And then there was the rest of the unpacking to keep her busy too.

When Diane finally got up, she pulled the bedroom curtains wide and looked out in the garden - her garden. It had been one of the many things that had made her fall in love with this house the first time she saw it. It wasn't a big garden, just enough for her to potter about and sit out in on warm days. Mark had never liked gardening and she'd given into his demands in the old house to pave over their garden and turn it into a drive for his car.

A clattering noise downstairs made Diane's heart jump. It would take a while to get used to the creaks and the groans of a new house. She peered over the bannister and at the bottom of the stairs could see a small pile of white envelopes by the front door. Wrapped up in her favourite, fluffy dressing gown, Diane headed downstairs to pick up the post. Some of it was addressed to her in her married name and those she kept to one side to deal with later. She'd already decided to make a start on reclaiming her own name as soon as she settled in. She looked around the living room, at the boxes that still cried out to be unpacked. Her fingers trailed along the top of a sealed box labelled 'Spare Room' and a smile spread across her face.

Diane ripped the tape from across the top of the box and greedily pulled the cardboard away to reveal the sewing machine inside. She pulled it out of the box and placed it on the carpet. The thoughts of becoming creative again, perhaps making her own curtains for the new house, made Diane smile even more.

She was brought out of her reverie by a sharp knock at the front door. Pulling her dressing gown tight around her, she opened the door just a crack and saw her neighbour, Susan at the door. She was carrying a plastic bag that was full to bursting with groceries.

"Just came to see if you're settling in all right?" Susan said, offering Diane the bag. "And I brought you this, just some bread and milk, teabags, that sort of thing. Sorry, I don't mean to intrude and I'm not usually this nosy, it's just that you seemed a bit… you know…. yesterday when you moved in."

Diane relaxed and opened the door fully, inviting Susan in. Diane walked into the living room and Susan followed.

"Yes, I was a bit… you know… yesterday," Diane laughed, waving a hand at the cardboard boxes. "But I'm looking forward to unpacking today."

Susan's eye was immediately caught by the sewing machine, standing in the middle of the living room floor.

"A sewing machine?" she cried. "Can you use it? Oh, please, tell me you can use it!"

"Why yes… I…" Diane began.

"We've been looking for someone who can sew!" Susan said. "Our theatre group, at the community centre, we're in desperate need of someone to help out with costumes. I mean, if you're interested, that is? Sorry, I didn't mean to sound pushy. I'm not usually so forward, honestly, I'm not. And I'm sure you're going to be busy and you might not have time to…"

Diane stopped her before she could say any more.
"I'd love to," she said. "I really would love to help out. Just give me a few days to settle in, get myself sorted out here, and then I'd be more than happy to help."

"There's a lot more going on, too, if you're interested, at the community centre," Susan suggested but then caught herself. "I'm sorry, I'm going too fast aren't I?"

Diane shook her head. "No, I appreciate it, really I do. Just give me a few days, I need to get used to this house. I want to enjoy sitting in the garden listening to the birds, I need to get used being on my own. But I'll let you know when I'm ready."

Diane looked into the plastic bag that Susan had brought.

"You say there's bread in here?" she asked.

Susan nodded. "And butter, and tea-bags. And I've brought a couple of mugs from home."

Diane walked over to her unpacked boxes and took out the toaster.

"Then the least I can do by way of thanks is make us some breakfast and you can tell me all about the theatre group and the clothes that need making."

"That's very kind of you," Susan replied.

Diane headed to the kitchen with the bag of groceries in one hand, the toaster in the other and a huge smile on her face.

"One slice or two?" she asked her new friend.

The Hoarder

"Looks like the weather forecast was right," Becky sighed, looking out into the dark of the day from the kitchen window. "It's pouring down, as predicted, and it looks like it's in for the day."

Tim glanced out of the window too.

"There's football on the telly later, so I've got a good excuse to stay in and watch it now," he smiled.

Becky resigned herself to a day stuck indoors.

"I might as well do some housework," she said.

"I'll give you a hand," Tim replied.

Becky glanced at her husband.

"Tell you what, Tim. If I do some cleaning, what do you say to sorting out the cupboard under the stairs?"

"But it doesn't need sorting out," Tim gulped. "I know where everything is in there."

"That's the problem!" Becky said. "You might know what's in there but I haven't a clue. It's chock-a-block with all your…"

She was going to say the word rubbish but decided on a more tactful approach.

"It's chock-a-block with all your bits and pieces and there's no room in there to store anything else."

"But… but it's…" Tim began to say but Becky cut him short.

"It's never been cleaned out since we moved into this house, Tim. All you've ever done is hoard things in there. I daren't even open the cupboard door for fear things will fall out and I'll not be able to get it shut again. I have no idea what half the stuff in there actually is."

"Now, just wait a minute, Becky. I think hoarding's rather a strong word," Tim said. "I store things, I admit that, but I'm not a hoarder. Every single thing that's in that cupboard is in there for a reason. It's all useful stuff - or at least it might come in useful one day."

"Hmm… we'll see," said Becky. "Look, it's still chucking down outside, so we might as well do some cleaning and sorting today. There's not much else we can do and I'm not going out in this weather. If we make a start on it now, we'll be finished well before the football starts and then I'll make us some cheese toasties to watch the match with."

"Oh, you know how to wind me around your little finger," smiled Tim, and he headed off into the hall.

Becky took the vacuum cleaner from the kitchen cupboard and plugged it in. She pulled the handle gently towards her and hit the big red button with her foot to start it up – but there was nothing. She tried again and again but still nothing. She unplugged it from the socket and plugged it in again, but when it still didn't start she knew she was beat.

"Flaming thing!" she yelled at the machine.

"What's that, love?" Tim yelled back from the hall.

"The vacuum cleaner won't start!" she said.

Tim walked into the kitchen to find Becky trying to dismantle the machine to see if she could find out why it wouldn't work. Without a word, he took in the make and model of it and went back to his cupboard under the stairs. Within minutes he was back with not only the instruction manual to their old machine, but a see-through bag containing all kinds of screws and bits of black plastic.

"Where on earth did you find that?" Becky asked, surprised to see the instructions for the old machine. "I thought we'd lost that years ago."

Tim gave a sideways nod and Becky glanced out into the hall where the door to the cupboard under the stairs was wide open.

"See, I told you some of the stuff in there was worth keeping," Tim smiled.

-0-

Half an hour later, Becky had vacuumed the downstairs carpets and polished the woodwork. It was when she was in the middle of cleaning the windows, that Tim came into the living room and suggested they both take a break.

"Fancy a cuppa?" he asked.

"Sounds great," Becky said. "But let me do it. If you're in the middle of sorting out your cupboard I don't want to stop you getting on with it all."

Tim walked back into the hallway and Becky followed her husband. But she stopped short when she saw the amount of old papers, bits of wood, bags and boxes of all shapes and sizes piled up in the hall. Tim disappeared back into the cupboard, intent on his work, while Becky edged past on her way to the kitchen.

"You all right in there?" she cried out to Tim. "I hope the reason you've piled all this stuff out here in the hall means it's going in the bin?"

But there was no reply from the cupboard, just a strange, muffled groan.

Becky switched on the kettle and busied herself preparing their pot of tea. She took their favourite mugs and laid them on a tray. Then she popped a few chocolate biscuits on a plate. Outside, the rain lashed against the window and Becky turned to watch as raindrops splashed up from the window sill. She turned quickly back to the tea-pot but caught it with her sleeve, bringing the whole thing crashing down to the floor.

"What on earth….?" Tim cried, rushing into the kitchen when he heard the noise.

Becky bent down to retrieve the teapot, which thankfully, was still in one piece. But the lid had smashed into shards.

"Here, let me," Tim said, picking up the pieces of the teapot lid and throwing them in the bin.

"We'll just have to make our tea in the cup," Becky said. "I know it's not ideal, but without a teapot we've got no choice."

A cheeky smile played around Tim's lips.

"I think I might just have the thing… " he said, and disappeared into the cupboard. When he returned this time, Becky burst out laughing when she saw what he had in his hands.

"How many are in there?" she laughed.

"About five, I reckon," Tim smiled. "I'm not sure if any of them will fit."

Becky reached into the clear plastic bag and pulled out a teapot lid, then another, and another, until five of them were lined up on the kitchen worktop.

"I remember this one!" she said, picking up a red teapot lid. "Didn't we get this teapot as a wedding present? But it started leaking, years ago, I remember, and we had to throw it away. And this striped one, wasn't that your…"

"…aunt Cath's, yes," Tim replied.

"And you've kept them all this time?" Becky shook her head in amusement.

"To be honest, I'd forgotten all about them," Tim admitted sheepishly. "I've just found them at the bottom of a box. But I think that blue one looks the right size to fit our tea pot."

Becky shot him a look.

"Once I've given it a good wash, of course," he added quickly.

"Is there anything else in that cupboard of yours you've found that you'd forgotten about?" Becky asked.

Tim cleared his throat.

"Well… there are a few… a few boxes of bits and pieces I was keeping in case we had to make do and mend things," he replied.

"Bu you are planning to throw some of this junk out, aren't you?" Becky said.

"Junk? Oh, you're a hard taskmaster, Becky Smith," Tim said. "One man's junk is another man's…"

"Junk," Becky said.

"… I was going to say treasure," Tim smiled. "But yes, I'll try to throw out as much as I can."

After their cup of tea served from a mismatched teapot, Tim went back to sorting out his cupboard while Becky dragged the vacuum cleaner slowly up the stairs. She was just about to plug the machine in to clean the bedroom carpets when she heard Tim loudly cry out.

"What is it?" she called out over the bannister.

After a minute or two, Tim appeared at the bottom of the stairs with a large, brown cardboard box in his hands.

"You'll never guess what I've found!" he said.

"What now?" Becky sighed. "More tea pot lids? The instruction manual to the food blender we got rid of in 1986? Oh no, let me guess – it's the first pair of shoes you wore to school and couldn't bear to get rid of?"

"Come down and see," Tim said. He heaved the box up and held tight until Becky had reached the bottom of the stairs.

"You might need to put some newspaper down on the table first, Becky, it's a bit dusty, this box."

Becky did as Tim suggested and then Tim carefully laid the battered, mucky old box on the paper. The tape holding the box closed had turned brittle and yellowed with age. The top flap of the box was open and Tim pulled it gently upwards so that Becky could take a peek inside.

"Looks like a load of old toy cars, to me," she said. "I hope you're going to chuck these out too."

Tim shook his head.

"You're right, Becky, they are old toy cars, but these are going nowhere near the bin."

"Why ever not?" she sighed.

"You remember the antiques programme we watched last weekend? The one where the young lad had been left old toys in his grandad's will?"

Becky thought for a moment, trying to recall the programme. She wasn't really interested in watching antiques on TV, but she knew Tim took a real interest.

"You must remember, Becky, it was the programme set near the castle we visited last summer, the one with the lovely tea shop on the lake?"

"Oh yes, I remember now," Becky nodded, thinking of the tea shop and its delicious salted caramel tart. "And what happened to this young lad's tin cars?" Tim's eyes glistened with excitement.

"They ended up being worth a small fortune," he said. "And he didn't have half as many as I've got in this box."

"But could you really bear to part with them and sell them?" Becky asked. "That doesn't sound like you. I thought you would have put the box back at the bottom of the cupboard and left it for another thirty years."

Tim sighed. "I'd forgotten I had these, Becky. They were passed down to me by my grandad Bill. I used to play with them when I was a lad, but then they've been sitting in this cupboard ever since we moved in here and went straight out of my mind."

"Our David wouldn't want them, would he?" Becky said, thinking of their son who was living down South.

Tim shook his head. "I've asked him in the past, but he's not interested."

Tim reached into the box and gently took out the old toys, one after the other. Some of them were scratched from years of being played. But many were in pristine condition, some even still in their boxes.

"I'm going to put them up for auction online," Tim declared. "After I've taken a whole load of the other stuff to either charity shops or the recycling centre."

"You really think you'll earn some money from selling these toys?" Becky asked.

"I do. I've seen these go for silly prices online, to real collectors, all over the world."

Becky smiled. "Any idea what you'll do with the money you'll earn?" she said.

"Well… I was thinking about buying a shed," Tim replied. "It'll free up the understairs cupboard and I can start to keep all of my …"

"Junk," Becky said.

"… all of my treasure outside in the shed."

"Good idea," said Becky as she planted a kiss on her husband's cheek.

Outside, the rain storm started to ease and the sun gently began to shine

The Holiday Camp

"It'll be fun!" I heard dad say on the phone to grandma Pat. "We're both looking forward to it, a lot," he said, then dad glanced at me and caught me listening in. "Can we talk about that later, Pat, please?" he said. As soon as dad hung up the phone, he slumped down on the sofa and let out a really long sigh.

"What's up, dad?" I asked him.

"Nothing, Kitten," he replied, shaking his head.

I glared at him, hard.

"Dad!" I cried. "You said…"

Dad laughed and held his hands up in mock surrender.

"I know, I know…you're too old to be called Kitten any more," he laughed. "But some old habits are hard to break."

Dad was the only one who still used my baby name, and he seemed to keep forgetting to call me by my proper name of Kitty. I tried not to be too upset with him when he used my baby name, because it was the name that mum used to call me, he said.

"Don't you want to go on holiday with grandma Pat and grandad Jack?" I asked dad.

"Going on holiday with them isn't the problem," he replied. "It's just…" and then he paused, as if he wanted to say more but felt that he couldn't, not in front of me.

"Well, let's just say I'm sure that the caravan will be nice and cosy with the four of us in it," he said. "At least the holiday park looks nice, Kitty. There are two swimming pools, a crazy golf course…"

"How do you know, dad?" I asked him.

He patted the seat on the sofa next to him. "Come here, love, I'll show you the website on the laptop and we can have a look around the holiday park online."

"Will we be able to see inside our caravan too?" I asked him.

"We might be able to…" dad said, clicking on the links in the website. He opened up a webpage for the Delta Deluxe caravan, which was the one grandma Pat had booked for us all. "That's it then, Kitty. Our home for the next fortnight," he said, moving the pointer on the screen around the inside of the caravan. "Although how the four of us are going to rub along together in there for two weeks is a mystery to me. It doesn't look like there's enough room to swing a cat," I heard dad mutter darkly.

"Only four of us? Is Sandra not coming with us, dad?" I asked him. I liked dad's new friend Sandra, she worked as a teacher in the next village to ours. She'd been coming over to our house for a few weeks now and both dad and I were really happy to have her in our lives.

"No, love," he said quietly. "Not this time. We'll see Sandra when we come home."

"We'll be all right in the caravan, dad," I smiled, as he looked a bit worried. "I'll look after you."

Dad ruffled my hair. "Thanks Kitten."

I gave him one of my looks; he'd forgotten again.

The next morning, dad woke me up early and after breakfast I helped bring my yellow holiday bag downstairs.

Dad brought our suitcases down and I watched from the living room window as he strapped one of the cases to the top of our car. With the house all locked up, we set off in the car to grandma Pat's and when we arrived, grandma and grandad were already standing outside their front door with their suitcases, waiting. Grandma Pat didn't look very happy, so I stayed in my seat in the back of the car behind dad's seat. Dad took their suitcases and put them in the boot of the car. Then grandad Jack sat next to dad in the front and grandma Pat sat next to me.

"Hello Kitty," she said, leaning in for a kiss. I kissed her back.

"Are you excited?" she asked me and I nodded my head.

"There are two swimming pools and a crazy golf course in the holiday park," I told her. "Although the caravan's not big enough to swing a cat, dad said."

I heard grandad Jack laugh from the front of the car as dad revved up the engine and we all set off on our journey to the Sunshine Holiday Park.

"I booked the best caravan that the park offers, you know, it's the Delta Deluxe. It's got not one, but two en-suites," grandma Pat sniffed, then she wound her window down. "Can I open a window?" she said, when the window was on its way down. "It's a bit stuffy in the back here."

"If she thinks this is stuffy, then heaven help us when we get to the caravan," I heard grandad Jack say to dad.

The car ride seemed to take forever, and we were all pretty quiet at the start. I was still really sleepy from being woken up so early that morning, but I was too excited to go to sleep.

It was mine and dad's first holiday together, with grandma and grandad. And it was the first time dad and I had ever been on holiday without mum. I knew that dad missed her, he talked about her all the time. Grandma Pat often cried when mum's name was mentioned and grandad Jack would lay his arm gently across her shoulder and pull her towards him into his arms. But I couldn't remember mum the way they all remembered her, I didn't have the memories that they all shared. All I had were photographs in frames on my bedroom wall, of mum with me as a baby in her arms, I would have liked, more than anything, more than I've ever admitted to dad, to have been able to remember her more.

After hours of dad's car trundling down the motorway, dad flicked the indicator lever to the left and we pulled off the main road into a service station car park. Grandad Jack was first out of the car, stretching his arms up into the air and yawning. After breakfast in the café, we all bundled back into the car, this time with dad in the passenger seat and grandad Jack at the wheel. I returned to the back seat with grandma, who still looked very sad. Grandad drove on for hours and by the time we arrived at the Sunshine Holiday Park it was almost time for tea. After checking in at the reception lodge, grandad drove slowly into the park following the directions to find our caravan. It didn't take long to unpack all the suitcases and get settled in. Grandma Pat said she would put the kettle on to make a pot of tea and grandad Jack asked if I'd like to go with him to the shops to buy milk.

I loved grandad Jack and always felt safe whenever I was with him. I felt I could talk to him about anything and so I asked him the question that had been bothering me all day.

"Why's grandma Pat looking so sad today, grandad?" He took a little while to reply, but finally he said quietly. "She's been thinking about your mum a lot over the last few weeks, Kitty. She loved her very much, you know."

We walked the rest of the way to the shop and back to the caravan in silence. But when we neared our caravan I could hear grandma Pat's raised voice as if she was shouting at someone.

"Don't you dare mention that woman's name to me again!" I heard her yell. Grandad Jack looked at me as if he was worried as we walked closer still to the caravan. "Your wife… my daughter… don't you ever forget that she's still part of our lives, part of our families!" grandma Pat yelled. "And you're admitting now to having a fling with some woman called Sandra?"

"It's not like that…" I heard dad say.

Grandad Jack rattled the caravan door before he went inside, and I followed. I saw grandma Pat sitting on the brown-checked seat around the little kitchen table and I could tell that she'd been crying. I looked at dad, who looked really upset too.

"Let's put the kettle on," grandad Jack said. "I think we could all do with a cuppa, right?"

"Kitty," dad said. "Do you want to go and finish unpacking in your room?"

"I've done it all, dad," I replied.

"No, Kitty," dad said, all stern-like. "Please, go and sort your things out in your room while I have a little chat with grandma Pat."

I knew that tone of voice, it was dad's way of saying he was not to be disobeyed and so I went to my room, sat on my bed and pulled out a book from my yellow holiday bag. I tried to read, I really did, but even though our caravan was the top of the range Delta Deluxe with its two en-suites, it had really thin walls.

"It's been over ten years," I heard dad say. "And in all that time, I've not so much as looked as another woman, not one. You know I loved Helen, Pat, there's nothing I wouldn't have done for her. And since she passed on, you know, both of you know, Kitty has been my whole life."
"You've done well by her too," I heard grandad Jack say. "She's a credit to you, Dave."
"But..." grandma Pat sobbed.
"Now, Pat," grandad Jack said. "Come on, love. Let the lad speak."
"I will never, ever forget Helen," dad said. "I wouldn't want to and I don't intend to. She will always be a part of my life, of Kitty's life too. Helen…" I heard dad's voice break before he started to speak again…"Helen will always be my first and true love. There is no-one… no-one who could ever replace her, you have to believe that, Pat."
"She does Dave," said grandad Jack softly. "She does."
I heard the whistle of the kettle and then a clinking of pots and spoons.
"I think we could do with some biscuits," grandad Jack said. "I'll just pop across to the shop for some." I heard the rattle of the door and felt the caravan shake a little as grandad Jack left. There was silence from the kitchen.

"Sandra is just a friend," I heard dad say eventually. "I like her - and Kitty likes her and, I'll be honest with you Pat because that's the only way I know how, I would like the friendship to develop, it's true. It's the first time I've felt this way about anyone since Helen..."

"I'm sorry, Dave," grandma Pat said. "Helen was our only child, you know."

"I know," dad said quietly. "I know. And you must also know that I'm not looking to replace her with someone else, I could never do that. But it's been ten years, Pat, I've worked hard and I've been a good dad to Kitty."

"You've been the best dad to Kitty," grandma Pat said. "It's just… it's going to take some getting used to, seeing you with another woman."

Just then, the caravan rocked slightly again as grandad returned.

"Chocolate shortbread biscuits all right for everyone?" he asked. "I think that pot of tea should be brewed by now if everyone's ready?"

"Are you ready?" I heard dad say, but I didn't know who he was asking as there was no reply, just a gentle sniffing noise. The caravan rocked gently again and I heard footsteps from the kitchen. Just then, there was a knock on my bedroom door. When it opened, dad popped his head in my room to see me.

"You can come out now, Kitten," he said.

This time, I didn't correct him about my name.

ABOUT THE AUTHOR

Glenda Young is author of the following books:

<u>NOVELS</u>

Belle of the Back Streets
Headline (2018)

The Tuppenny Child
Headline (2019)

Pearl of Pit Lane
Headline (2019)

<u>SHORT STORY COLLECTIONS</u>

Just the Ticket
(2019)

Help! My Husband's a Hipster
(2019)

The Sea glass Collector
(2016)

<u>TELEVISION TIE-IN BOOKS</u>

Coronation Street: The Official Colouring Book
Hamlyn / Octopus Publishing Group Ltd (2016)

Deirdre: A Life on Coronation Street
Century / Random House / ITV Publishing (2015)

A Perfect Duet. The diary of Roy and Hayley Cropper
An unofficial Coronation Street companion book
FBS Publishing e-book and paperback (2014)

Norman Bates with a Briefcase. The Richard Hillman
Story
An unofficial Coronation Street companion book
KDP e-book (2014) and CreateSpace paperback
(2016)

Coronation Street: The Complete Saga
Updated from 2008-2010 (ITV / Carlton Publishing
2010)

Coronation Street: The Novel
Updated from 2003-2008 (ITV / Carlton Publishing
2008)

Editor of Coronation Street fan websites:
Coronation Street Blog
http://coronationstreetupdates.blogspot.com

Corrie.net
http://www.corrie.net

Please visit my website at
http://glendayoungbooks.com

First published in April 2019 by Glenda Young

Printed in Great Britain
by Amazon

82716433R00068